The Perfect Match

Karen Tucci

True Heart Romance

Contents

Note from the Author

To Read or Not to Read?

That is a question only you can answer. I've discovered that revealing some of the harsh topics discussed in this book up front is controversial. First, I will admit that I forget these warnings all the time. Not on purpose or out of disrespect, but because I wrote the book and lived in it for the last few months, I tend to be immune to things by the time it is published. Second, I believe everyone is capable of managing themselves. I don't need to do that for them. If a topic in a book bothers me, I can add it to my DNF (Did Not Finish) list, and that's okay. Third, I still have a book hanging out on my Kindle that I return to periodically. I found it more challenging to read once I read the trigger warning because I wasn't enjoying the story; I was waiting for those parts of the story to appear.

That said, I understand the reasoning behind the other side of the debate. Some people need to prepare themselves to read a book that might bring up a struggle they endured in the past.

In an effort to support all readers, I will list the challenging topics in this flirty, marriage of convenience, suspenseful ranch romance on the next page. If you want to read it, it is available. If you prefer to avoid such lists, skip the next page.

Either way, I wrote this for readers to enjoy Damon and Harlyn's coming together as they deal with their pasts.

Blessings,

Karen

Warning List

Kidnapping

Controlling and manipulative parent/child relationship

Karen's Other Books:

Stand Alone Books:

<u>When the Dust Settles: A Sweet Romance with a Navy SEAL</u>

G & G Security Series (Coming 2025)

(The characters from When the Dust Settles cross-over in this series)

Operation: Heal my SEAL Book 1

Operation: Find my SEAL Book 2

Operation: Keep my SEAL Book 3

Operation: Train my SEAL Book 4

Second Chance Series:

<u>Starting Over</u>

<u>Moving On</u>

Big L' Ranch Series

<u>The Perfect Kiss: Book 1</u>

<u>The Perfect: Cowboy Book 2</u>

<u>The Perfect Match Book 3</u>

<u>The Perfect Christmas (Holiday Novella)</u>

<u>The Perfect Sheriff Book 5</u>

Best Friends Series

<u>Let Me Carry You</u>

<u>Let Me Marry You</u>

YA Cumberland Christian Prep School Series

The Big Score (Coming 2025)

Chapter 1

"*Hunker down, let your feet burn in that fire, and when the fire is snuffed out, you'll come out smelling like your favorite flower.*"

Did she still believe her pastor's words even though he hadn't believed her? In short, yes. Pastor Jim spoke biblical truths. He never watered God's word down or found ways to make sin okay by plucking a line or two from the Bible completely out of context.

Why hadn't he believed me? Things would have been very different for Harlyn if someone had believed her all those years ago.

She understood her teachers' and headmaster's dismissals. Harlyn's parents had funded their jobs and programs at the school—she definitely couldn't mess that up.

But her pastor? Even the youth group pastor had disengaged. He'd gone so far as to ask her to stop attending the group, fearing her parents would "get wind of the lies she was spreading and shut him down."

For the past ten years, Harlyn had lived out of the motorhome her Grandpa gifted her so she could get away. Unfortunately, Brockton was too stupid to move on. She knew that wasn't true. He was an intelligent man, but something wasn't adding up. He pursued her even though he could have nearly any woman he wanted. Brockton was attractive on the outside. Dark hair that was tapered on the sides, very business-like, matching his hot cocoa eyes. His shoulders, lean and tone, led to healthy biceps—vanity muscles since he wouldn't know manual labor if it kicked him in the rear.

Today was the tenth anniversary of her Grandpa's death. Sticking with tradition, she visited their secret burger joint. Just in time—her stomach was begging for food. Her grandparents had snuck her there every chance they could.

Memories flooded her mind, reminding her of all the pain, hurt, and distress in her life. The most recent distress came when she found what she thought her Grandpa left her as the answer to her ultimate freedom ended up only being paperwork. With her bodyguard's help, she'd discovered the title and bill of sale for the motorhome, copies of her Grandparents' wills, documentation from Grandpa's family that she didn't understand, and all Richard, her attorney, who'd also been Grandpa's before he died, told her was that she was getting closer. *How frustrating.*

"Thank you." Harlyn grabbed her burger and drink from the young girl. Envy was a dangerous and wasted emotion, yet looking at the worker in front of her, so full of life, ripped at Harlyn's insides.

She'd been delusional enough as a young girl to think she could do anything she wanted. Yes, things seemed to be working out well for Harlyn now, but she was nearly thirty. She'd missed out on her younger years.

Growing up in the wealthiest family in Wilshire, Connecticut. Living on the state's Gold Coast in a seventeen-million-dollar home wasn't as glamorous as one would think. Harlyn had become her parent's target when she started questioning their behavior and motives.

She'd prayed the Lord would heal her one day. More than healing for herself, she'd wanted God to punish them. Their manipulation of everyone and everything within their circle made her stomach churn. People compromised their own beliefs so the Summers power couple, AKA her parents, wouldn't destroy them. People tolerated their cunning words and misguided behaviors because they didn't believe these two prominent people would be anything but gracious and generous with their resources.

Come on, people! Wake up! She'd said those words to herself a decade ago, right before she left her parents' home, enacting her Grandpa's plan.

The surveillance camera in the corner caught her attention as she left the fast food establishment, riddling her with heinous memories she prayed she would forget.

Who puts cameras in their daughter's bedroom to make sure she is doing what they want? "Yours," her inner self responded with a dose of reality. *Who locks their daughter away when she disagrees with their thinking?* "Yours again." *Shut up!* She chastised herself.

As hardened and bitter as her feelings were for her parents, pastors, and "friends" who'd walked away when she revealed her hard times, she didn't want God to be disappointed in her, so Harlyn continued to pray, hoping He'd helped her release that bitterness. Every day, she made the choice to be happy.

The song, *Daylight*, popped into her head as she walked to her vehicle through the parking lot shared with a small grocery store. Blurting out a line or a chorus here or there never embarrassed Harlyn. "You saved my life, not once but twice . . . you make sure I always see the daylight. . . It's amazing what the hard times will reveal, like who shows up, who walks away, and who's for real. So take me on, I'll take the wheel, and we can both outrun the past . . ."

Harlyn opened her eyes and saw a gaggle of people watching her singing performance. Who hasn't seen a drinking straw be a microphone before?

Giggling, she waved, "'Daylight' by Shinedown, gotta love it."

Some would say she was delusional, thinking she could outrun Brockton. Even so, she'd never give up. She needed to win or pay with her life. Harlyn decided long ago that *winning* meant she stayed out of her parents and Brockton's clutches.

A sudden fear crawled up her throat, clamping her windpipe shut when a car caught her eye. *Oh, dear God, don't let that be him!* Harlyn's chest tightened as she ran and ducked below the driver's window on the driver's side, hoping the black Mercedes Benz drove by.

"Phew, that was close," she let out her clogged breath and pressed her hand to her rapidly moving chest.

In truth, Harlyn's paranoia was working over time. She'd cut all her body-guards loose a week ago. It'd been six months since she'd had her last glimpse of Brockton. He snapped a picture of her with his phone, got in his car and drove away. Something about that continued to plague at the back of Harlyn's mind. *All these years, why hadn't he tried to capture her?* She certainly wasn't complaining—she had not signed up for this game of Manhunt. Harlyn shuddered, recalling the one time he'd gripped her wrist, but her bodyguards protected her.

She'd enjoyed living independently for the last ten years and being responsible for her well-being and livelihood. Sometimes, she seemed like a fraud. Living off the money her grandfather gave her, she would never have to work another day, but she wouldn't do that. Harlyn wanted more.

Photography was her happy place. Twice, she won the Prix Pictet under her pseudonym, J.C.L.H. The first one was a black-and-white photo of a little girl happily eating an ice cream in perfect focus. In the background, that same little girl was crying, hugging her knees to her chest as the adults, presumably her parents, just watched. The father, staring off as if he had someplace else to be, and the mother looked like a cross between Cruella de Vil and Lady Tremaine. The second was a bird's eye view of the Sonoran Desert, showing the vibrant life that exists during the spring.

Upon reflection, Halryn loved how she could capture the dreadfulness of her childhood in her first winning and the flourishing of life in her second, something she hoped her future held for her.

At one time, it'd been her goal to win a Pulitzer. That all changed when Harlyn visited a farm shortly after she settled in Arizona. The family worked endlessly to feed their customers. There was a lot to farming, and her desire to learn took over. Obtaining her degree in Agronomy, God filled her with tranquility.

Harlyn hopped into her RV and quickly ate her lunch, finishing just in time for her job interview via video call for an agricultural expert on a farm in Montana. Well, that's what she thought it was until Amelia, the owner, revealed the hundreds of thousands of acres Harlyn would be living on and partially responsible for. *Yikes!* It was nothing like the Knight's Farm in Arizona.

"You won't be the only person obligated to care for the gardens and orchards at first. Damon also has his degree and will help get you acclimated," Amelia explained.

Living on a working ranch, not a farm, would help Harlyn regain some semblance of normalcy. She'd loved traveling the country, taking photos, winning awards, and meeting people, but it was lonely. Not lonely enough to return to Connecticut, she wanted regular human interaction.

She'd be the big three-oh in a few short months. Harlyn wanted more—a family, one that she chose, that she loved. One she'd cherish and shower with love.

"Why do you think I should hire you?" Amelia asked her.

I don't her mind screamed, but refrained from sharing.

A few moments of silence made Halryn's pulse pick up speed. *The truth will set you free.*

"I'm not sure I do." Harlyn paused, waiting to see if Amelia would respond, but she didn't. "I got my degree over two years ago and haven't had an opportunity to use it. God kept telling me to be still." She huffed a laugh that earned her a chuckle on the other end of the line.

"I planned on working at a farm in Arizona, but tough times hit them. I offered to volunteer, but they wouldn't hear of it because we'd grown close."

Harlyn took in a silent breath before continuing. "My heart keeps telling me that the farm inspired me to get my degree, but God has bigger plans for me, and maybe God has been preparing me for your massive ranch."

Silence filled the air. Halryn checked her screen to make sure the call hadn't dropped.

"I'd like to offer you the position for this season. We'll see how you fit in and go from there. How does that sound?" Amelia offered.

Without hesitation, Harlyn blurted out, "I can be there in two days."

"Perfect. You'll be here for the End of Summer Festival. It will be a fun way to meet everyone."

Amelia shared the ranch address, prayed for traveling mercies, and bid her farewell.

"She is my kind of person," Harlyn cheered out loud.

Already refueled, RV and belly respectively, Harlyn turned over the engine and began her journey again, this time toward a more permanent residency, Haven Ridge, Montana.

"Big L' Ranch, here I come."

Chapter 2

Damon Richards struggled to be positive sometimes, and today was one of those days. This morning, Darlene cried when he put her hair in a ponytail because he couldn't do the French braid she requested. He'd tried, but it'd turned into a twirled mess.

Later, Reneé texted about the kids' lunches. He'd forgotten them. Today was the rare day when Cash and Carolyn weren't available at lunchtime, so everyone brought their own. He'd thought he'd been doing fine raising the kids alone, but lately, Damon was failing—just like Cheryl said he would.

Speaking of being a failure, he stared at the empty wall in the horse barn designated for the wild horses he trained and the beautiful mare, Meadow—saddle bronc rider, Tanner Brooks's ticket to another Gold Buckle, hopefully.

It'd been eight long years since Damon had hung up his saddle. His ex-wife had finally gotten what she wanted—Damon quit.

This decision had been a turning point in his life, marking the end of his rodeo career and, unbeknownst to him, the beginning of his journey as a single father.

Damon grabbed Meadow's brush from the wall and ran it down her back, flattening out the matted hair from the saddle.

A few weeks ago, his rodeo buddy, Tanner Brooks, unexpectedly arrived at the ranch, begging Damon to train his new horse, Meadow, for nationals. Tanner's long-time horse, Shadow, had to be put down due to an injury. With only a few months before the NFR, Damon hoped Meadow could bring home the Stock of the Year award to match Brooks's Gold Buckle, which he was sure to win.

He squashed the longing in his heart whenever he thought about competing. Some pain came from giving up the sport he loved, but most of the ache ran deeper, and he stuffed that down—far.

"Hey, Buddy!" Tanner exploded into the barn; nothing uncommon for his personality.

"I don't know how you do it." Tanner slapped him on the back.

"Do what?" Damon's voice sounded uninterested.

"Live on this ranch with that woman," he rested his elbows on the wood behind him, dipping his chin and pointing toward Harlyn, the newest employee at Big L' Ranch, "and not start something with her?"

To Damon, Harlyn seemed distant, always on alert, and rarely on time, annoying him, but his kids loved her. Go figure. Even if he were interested in starting anything with her, which he wasn't, he didn't trust easily, and unless they were arguing about *the right way* to tend the crops, he was tongue-tied.

That said, he wasn't oblivious. Damon's head pounded, thinking about how cute she was when she sang her songs randomly throughout the day. He refused to comment on how she was a knockout in jeans and a T-shirt; both hugged her soft curves perfectly. He fell victim to her green eyes, especially when a strip of her red hair fell down, and she blew a hard breath up, trying to remove it from her line of vision.

Studying Damon, Tanner chortled, "Don't feed me any bologna that you're not interested in her. Every ranch hand from here to the Rockies has called Amelia asking to take them on just to be close to her."

"Really?"

"Gotcha." He pointed at his buddy. "Why don't you just go after her?"

"You know why."

Tanner had "buckle bunnies" following him from one rodeo to another. That was never Damon's scene. He'd focused on Gold Buckles, not the women. He didn't want one who'd pick up and leave at the drop of a cowboy hat. That's why he chose Cheryl. Ha, the joke was on him.

"You'll never change. Chasing women wherever you go," Damon chuckled.

"Hey," Tanner puffed out his chest. "I don't chase them. They come flocking to me."

"Good grief!" Damon fed Meadow an apple while Tanner moved, brushing the other side of her. "So, are you losing your touch? She doesn't seem to notice you." Damon nudged his head toward Harlyn.

The stupid grin filling Tanner's face caused Damon to cringe. Tanner wouldn't think twice about embarrassing him.

"You have been out of the game way too long." Backhanding Damon's shoulder, Tanner cursed. "Dude, I can read women!"

Unable to stop himself, Damon's howling laughter spread throughout the barn, disrupting the horses.

Tanner yelled above him. "Laugh now, but mark my words. That woman's eyes scream, *I want Damon!*"

Damon loved the fall months. It was mid-Friday afternoon, and the temperature was still seventy-five degrees. However, the sun descended quicker this time of year, and the closer it got to the horizon, the faster the warm temperature would disappear with the light.

As the men gathered at the picnic table, Tanner invited Harlyn to join the guys-only break. Even worse, he slid over and offered her the seat between him and Damon.

"I'm sure she's too busy to sit with us," Damon said gratingly.

No offense, but he'd seen enough of her today and still had to work in the orchard with her, so having her sit almost on top of him now was too much.

"Do the kids and Renee come outside for a break, or is it just. . . you guys? I don't mean that rudely. I'm just wondering."

Quinton chuckled. "It's just us."

"I'll have to take a rain check. I'm meeting with the kids after lunch and need to prepare. They will help us wrap the apple trees for the winter."

By us, she'd meant herself and Damon. He'd been selected to help out the new woman as long as she needed. His eyes were fixed on her jeans and undershirt, which fit like second skin. She covered the shirt with a flannel two sizes too big and tied in front. It had slipped off her shoulder earlier, and the spaghetti strap holding her shirt caught his eye as it rested on her tanned, toned shoulder.

He understood the reasoning behind him helping out Harlyn. Damon had grown up on a ranch. He followed in his dad's footsteps, training and competing while his mom showed him how to tend a mean garden.

Damon dared to lift his eyes, meeting Harlyn's for a brief moment before looking back down at the table. Since Tanner infected his thoughts earlier in the day that Harlyn liked him, he'd watched her intently but kept his distance.

What was he twelve? No. But he sure felt like it. Only Tanner and Raddix knew Damon's turmoil. His pain stemmed from his insecurity that he had done something wrong, causing Cheryl to leave his kids motherless and half of his bed cold.

Had he ever thought of getting remarried? Yes. Love wasn't at the top of his list of reasons, though. The desire for companionship and a mother for his kids continued to etch at his mind.

The women on the ranch were great, but Darlene repeatedly mentioned wanting her mom to live with them, help her pick out her clothes, make her breakfast, and do her hair.

As Darlene got older, she would need her mother, and since Cheryl didn't have any interest in being part of their little family, shouldn't he make sure his children had a mother?

"Everyone needs to eat," Tanner's voice, trying to persuade Harlyn to stay, jolted Damon back to the conversation.

"Maybe next time. I'm heading to town for a quick errand." Harlyn's smile could have filled Central Montana twice." Then, Darlene asked to partner with me when we wrapped. She is so excited, and I don't want to disappoint her."

"That sounds like fun," Tanner's voice piqued, eyeing Damon.

"I bet she is. It's been a long time since she's had a mother figure take this much interest in her," Raddix added.

Damon knew Raddix was saying that to stir up trouble. The women on the ranch had been great with his kids.

"O-oh, no, no. I'm not that for Darlene." Haryln stammered out.

Damon took in the sight of her slowly deepening cotton candy pink cheeks. He wanted to agree, but he hadn't seen Darlene this invested in anyone, so he clenched his jaw, keeping his thoughts silent.

"She's just excited for a new face on the ranch." Harlyn jerked her thumb toward the main house. "I have to get going."

Harlyn strutted away. It was not like she was trying to gain the men's attention; it was her normal gait—one that pulled Damon's attention away many times before.

"I told you," Tanner bellowed, fist-pumping Raddix.

Damon dropped his sandwich. "What?" His hands slapped against the table. "You're siding with the opposition?" He accused Raddix.

"I am. This is payback. Remember how funny you thought it was when I'd fallen for Lily but was still too hung up on my three-date rule." The recollection dawned on Damon. "That's why I decided to team up with Tanner when he brought it to my attention that Harlyn has the hots for you."

Quinton chuckled before he could take a bite of his sandwich. "It doesn't look like Harlyn's the only one with feelings."

Damon laid into him. "Of all people, you should understand."

He felt terrible when Quinton put his sandwich down. "You can't help when someone leaves you, whether through death like my late wife or through divorce. If you choose to stay broody and miserable for the rest of your life, that's your choice. I like having a warm bed at night."

That shut Damon up. Quinton smirked and picked up his bread. "Now I am going to eat the sandwich *my wife* made me."

Low blow, Quin.

"We don't even know if she likes me. Tanner thinks every woman likes him. Wait until he stops winning the Gold Buckles, and then we'll see how many truly adore him."

"It doesn't matter if she likes you. Well, it does, but how do you feel?" Tanner grilled him.

He wasn't ready to admit this, but Harlyn had stirred up emotions he never thought he'd feel again.

Lily and Amelia sauntered toward the picnic table, greeting Raddix and Quinton, respectively, with quick kisses that Damon remembered and longed for.

"Whatcha talking about?" Lily asked casually.

None of the men answered. Instead, they all looked toward Damon, obviously hoping he'd say something.

"No worries," Amelia crooned. "We can get all the gossip during pillow talk tonight."

Lily giggled in agreement.

Damon knew they were right. What man could resist his wife?

Raddix and Lily had eloped a couple of weeks ago after getting word that her stalker had a history of harassing other women. He'd be behind bars for decades. He wrapped his arm through Lily's legs, resting his palm just above her knee. "Dude, you're going to lose this one." He looked up at his new wife with a tenderness he had for none other. "Without question."

"Just tell them," Damon said, stuffing his sandwich in his mouth.

Once the women were abreast of the situation, they scattered like mice, probably to stir up trouble for him.

"Sorry, Man. Lily has taken a liking to Myrtle."

The mere mention of one-third of the Troublesome Trio set alarms off inside Damon's head. They liked to meddle in everyone's business. Hazel helped her husband, Frank, run the diner when he needed help. The trio used the diner as their hangout as if they were still teenagers, and they seemed to know everything happening in town. His kids loved eating at the diner. He knew it was only a matter of time before those ladies focused on him.

The trio had been trying to arrange dates for him, but he always refused. Then, to their surprise, Damon had participated in the town's first bachelor auction in July when Quinton had proposed to Amelia, and Lily paid three thousand dollars for a date with Raddix, beating out the eight hundred dollars Damon brought in. His buddy still had a few months of their side bet, allowing Raddix any time off he wanted before the end of the year.

Damon lost his self-confidence when Cheryl left, but thanks to Tanner, Raddix, and Quinton, his mind started questioning everything. Could it be possible that Harlyn found him appealing just the way he was? Probably not. Did it matter? No. He'd never put himself through that again. One date to help raise money for the town was one thing, but actually dating, or worse, getting married again. Never!

Chapter 3

Willow had overbooked herself at the salon today. Ever since Val and her sister, Harper, left for a short vacation, Willow had been booked solid.

Today that left Harlyn in the same room with one-third of the Troublesome Trio while Willow transformed Harlyn from a redhead to a blonde.

"So tell me about yourself, Dear," Doris yelled in Harlyn's direction, drowning out the sound of the hair dyer in Willow's hand.

Willow squeezed Harlyn's shoulder. That was her warning—share with caution. Doris was the second most dangerous of the Troublesome Trio. She fell slightly behind Myrtle. If this were the Olympics, Mrytle would earn a gold medal for getting into everyone's business and knowing everyone's information.

That analogy had come straight from Lily. While Harlyn loved everyone on the ranch, she spent most of her time with Reneé, helping with the kids during school, Lily and Katy. Lily was like the sister she never had, and Katy was the mother she always wished she had.

Harlyn wasn't too worried about the older women. Doris was so friendly. "I came to work for Amelia at Big L' Ranch. When I arrived, the town had its End of the Summer Festival. I love this place and the people."

She assumed this was not the information Doris sought, but Harlyn wasn't willing to share anything else right now.

"Especially that hunk, Damon. Hubba Hubba. Those lean muscles, tough, rugged look." Doris fanned herself. "He gets the blood flowing, doesn't he, Dearie?"

Oh, dear God, please help me! This woman worked hard to appear young but was in her seventies. She shouldn't be dissecting a man in his thirties. Willow and Harlyn burst out laughing.

"You just wait until you're my age. If you never marry like me, you'll also observe all the young hunks." Doris fluffed and primed her hair.

She wasn't wrong. Damon was all those things, but she didn't want to hear Doris's thoughts. Harlyn had enough of her own, causing her fitful night's sleep. She'd admired his thick arms, chocolate eyes, and the care he took with his kids.

Harlyn cringed when thinking about never marrying. On the one hand, that sounded perfect since she was betrothed to Brockton, and she'd already decided it would be over her dead body that she'd marry him.

However, she longed for a decent man to care about her, love her, have the pillow talk Lily and Amelia swooned about, and kiss. He had the perfect lips for kissing—full, smooth, and irresistible whenever he smiled. She'd taken a picture. Yes, the adage about a picture lasting longer definitely applied to Damon and his smile. Damon could be her man if he weren't so hot and cold. And if she didn't have her past to deal with.

Yesterday, he was a grump the entire time he helped winterize the greenhouse. Once they'd finished, she'd thought he was examining her with an intrigued eye. He even gazed at her lips but then stomped away, muttering under his breath.

His actions told Harlyn that Damon had zero interest in a relationship, so she hadn't let her mind wander further down that path.

Brockton had been the one and only person she'd kissed. Ironically, she'd compared him to kissing a snake at the time. To be fair, they were teens, but even she knew not to gag the other person with her tongue. *Geesh.*

Now, everything about Brockton, not just his kissing, reminded her of a snake. She prayed every night that his pompous, preppy self would never find her again.

"Did you leave a special someone behind?" Doris pried, pulling Harlyn from her thoughts.

"Special? Not."

"Hmm."

"Oh, no. Watch out for this one," Willow interjected. "Nothing embarrasses her. In fact, I think she gets a kick out of embarrassing others."

"Not true," Doris squeaked.

Willow harrumphed. "Says the woman who locked the sheriff and me in the tool shed at the church."

"What!?"

"Yeah, we went out of our way to help clean up after the festival, brought everything back to the church, and put it away. Doris and her troublesome friends locked us in."

"The wind blew the doors shut, Dear—"

"—Yep, and put the bar across the doors. Two hours we were stuck in there."

"Oh, cry me a lifetime of Manna." Doris dabbed her fake tears.

"I was locked in a shed with the most handsome sheriff around," she mocked Willow. "Haven't you had the biggest crush on that man for the last couple of years, and aren't you looking for a husband?" Doris lifted her eyebrows, waiting for a response.

Willow's high cheekbones were now watermelon-pink.

"Ah, there's a story here," Harlyn sang." Pulling her key necklace tight while Willow continued to blow dry her hair.

Ignoring Harlyn, Willow yelled over the noise. "That's pretty. What's it go to?"

"Not exactly sure, but it means a lot to me. It's a gift from my grandparents."

There couldn't have been a better moment for Sheriff McDugal to grace the ladies with his presence. With the twinkling of an eye, he entered the salon. Everyone hushed.

Willow turned off the hair dryer. The grin on his face let the ladies know that he'd heard the conversation. His eyes roamed back and forth between Willow and Harlyn, then Doris. The corners of his mouth turned up, and he shook his head. He probably knew all too well how dangerous this woman was.

"Willow, I just dropped in to see if you could cut my hair tomorrow."

"The only spot I have available is six."

"I'll take it. Thank you."

"Are you on day duty, Sheriff?" Doris inquired.

"Yes, Ma'am."

"Ohh, that's perfect." She directed her following statement toward Willow. "Once you get the sheriff looking even more handsome than he already is, he can take you to dinner. Frank and Hazel will be happy to see you."

Harlyn bit the inside of her cheek to prevent herself from laughing. *Doris was ruthless.*

The sheriff's pink cheeks matched Willow's as he shifted back and forth but quickly recovered. "I think that's a great idea, Willow?"

"S-sure," Willow stammered. "I'll see you tomorrow."

If the sheriff had left any quicker, Harlyn would have missed it.

"Doris, you have to stop interfering in people's lives," Willow burst out.

"Why? You've been pining over him for however long. I at least got you dinner; the rest is up to you."

Her blasé attitude about the situation made Harlyn laugh.

"Find my situation comical?" Willow released the chair to the ground, shaking out Harlyn's new blonde hair.

"Hopefully, you'll find it just as funny when it's your turn."

"My turn? I haven't done anything to anyone."

"And I have?" Willow looked offended, but Harlyn had learned some of this woman's facial features since she'd arrived and knew Willow rarely got upset.

Turning her attention to Doris. "Harlyn does have a point, though. Why don't you focus on someone like Selena."

Doris pushed out a hard breath. "I'm not a miracle worker." She pointed her perfectly painted hot pink nail at Willow. "You're meant to be with our hunky sheriff, and you," she pointed at Harlyn, "I see you with a handsome cowboy."

If only her grandpa had been as blunt with her as Doris was, she might already be married to a great man and safe from the clutches of her parents and Brockton.

I miss you, Grandpa!

Chapter 4

Once she returned from Willow's, Harlyn spent the next two hours ripping weeds from the bases of each tree and insulating them with wood chips. This would prevent the roots from freezing, keep the soil moist, and suppress new weeds.

Being out of the northeast brought her a sense of calmness and a slower-paced life. She'd heard theories that New Englanders were always on the go preparing for the next season, especially winter.

They had pretty severe winters here in Montana, too, but the people weren't agitated, snarling at each other, trying to get their tasks done.

Instead, everyone worked together, as the Bible suggests. *Many hands make like work*. Harlyn could get used to this surreal way of life.

Just as Reneé let the kids out of school for the day, she gushed over Harlyn's new hair color. Then, she left the kids with Harlyn, who'd recently finished the prep work and was thrilled to have help wrapping the trunks.

"We don't have to wrap them, you know," Damon said again, arguing with her about this for the umpteenth time.

Harlyn locked her eyes with his and let out an exasperated sigh. "Yes, I heard you. They are over five years old and don't need to be wrapped." She'd heard his textbook answer loud and clear.

"Fine, let's paint them white then. We need the sun's reflection during the winter to help them. You either paint them or wrap them." She crossed her arms over her chest, jutted her hip, and waited.

His lips tightened, and his eyes narrowed, challenging her to call him out again.

No problem.

"With Emmanuel and Lily having Crohn's, we should take every precaution possible and not use paint if, by chance, that caused a problem for them."

She gripped her hips. "Clearly, besides being a horse whisperer and an agricultural guru, you're also a doctor and know that the paint will be fine. Pretty impressive." The edginess of her tone even surprised her.

Where had that verbal diarrhea come from?

"Horse whisperer?" he mouthed to the kids, who were staring at him, waiting to see if he would respond. They all shrugged their shoulders.

"What's a horse whisperer?" Emmanuel asked.

"Someone really good with horses; understands them perfectly." His eyes met hers and softened at the compliment.

Lily, Katy, Renee, and Amelia were razzing her about Damon during lunch. Of course, she thought he was attractive. Even a blind woman could see how sickly handsome this man was with his strong jaw, a voice that could melt marshmallows and hair that begged Harlyn's hands to run her fingers through. What really got her were his hazel eyes. When they met hers, her insides turned into boiling soup. If she wanted to keep her brain intact, she shouldn't even acknowledge his full, rather tempting lips. She most definitely would have accepted their invitation had there been one.

For now, she needed to play nice, not pay attention to the handsome cowboy invading her mind, and create space between them before she did something stupid. Thank goodness the kids were here to keep her focused.

"There you go, start at the bottom and wrap it around from the bottom, making sure you overlap the paper," Harlyn instructed the kids.

Dean and Emmanuel worked on one tree while Dominic and Damon worked on the neighboring tree. Darlene was waiting for Harlyn to help with her tree. Of course, it had to be the one next to Damon.

Harlyn knelt too close to Damon and lost her balance. Naturally, Damon didn't move when she bumped him. He wasn't as thick as Quinton or Raddix but tall and all muscle.

"Are you okay?" Damon tossed her an amused look over his shoulder. As if he had a second thought about being a better role model for his kids, he stood and stuck his hand out in her direction.

She didn't want or need his help. "I'm good, thanks." It might have come out more snarky than expected, but she never wanted to be someone's afterthought.

Thankfully, she had her sweet romance novels to use as a guide. Although male heroes may not exist perfectly in the real world, she hoped that there were men who resembled the characters. She wouldn't settle for less than she deserved.

Darlene handed her the paper, and they started wrapping it together. Harlyn was impressed with the dedication the young girl put into her job. The boys were already complaining about how long this would take.

"We're not doing all the trees today," Harlyn assured them.

When the boys cheered, she lifted her eyes just in time to see Damon fist-bumped them. "You are just a big boy." Harlyn refused to admit how cute Damon was with the kids.

Invading her space, Damon stepped forward, and his lips were at her ear, causing her pulse to spike. He spoke into her hair, "There's nothing *boy* about me."

Her breath hitched, rendering her oxygen-deprived. Tingles fluttered throughout her body. She'd like to blame them on the cooling temperatures but didn't see the point in lying to herself.

Damon returned to his tree to finish wrapping while she remained frozen like an idiot. *How could he be so blasé?*

The more he interacted with Harlyn, the more hero-like qualities she saw in him. Her man didn't need a cape or iron-clad costume. He needed to make her stomach plummet and her heart race with the words he spoke and his proximity.

"You're really pretty," Darlene pulled Harlyn back to the task with a sweetness to her voice.

"Come on, Darlene," Dean complained, scrunching his nose.

Dominic stopped mid-wrap. "Dad, why do girls go around telling each other they are pretty?"

Damon opened his mouth to speak, but Harlyn beat him to it. "Usually, it's because the guys don't tell her enough."

That shut them all up. Harlyn inwardly rejoiced when they stared at each other with questioning eyes.

A hot minute passed, and Damon spoke up, "You know, boys, it could also be because some women are too stubborn to hear or accept a compliment when given one."

Now it was on. "Is that so?" Harlyn stood with her hands on her hips.

"Yes, it is. A man can tell a woman how beautiful she looks, and she'll brush it off or say he doesn't mean it."

Harlyn crossed her arms over her chest. "Sounds like you have experience. Perhaps if your compliments weren't afterthoughts, they'd be taken more seriously."

"What's that supposed to mean?"

"Hey, guys. Stop fighting. Let's just wrap the trees," Emmanuel spoke up, looking nervous with his hands over his ears.

Emmanuel's well-being trumped winning a silly argument with a pigheaded man any day. They returned to their trees like siblings scolded by their parents for arguing. The zings fluttering through her body were far from brotherly feelings.

It hadn't taken her long to get in Emmanuel's good graces once he knew how much she loved the Marvel movies. Harlyn had been helping Reneé during school hours once she finished her agricultural responsibilities. Dean and Dominic talked with her daily while Darlene cozied up to her. They even let her take pictures of them. Harlyn had it all—safety, photography, friends, and a slight crush on an annoying cowboy.

By the time they quit for the evening, they'd wrapped two rows of trees, and Harlyn was ready for a shower and something quick to eat.

She appreciated eating at the main house every night. Cash and Carolyn were even better chefs than the ones her mother breezed through during Harlyn's childhood. Though lively conversation and friendliness around the table were foreign to her, she welcomed them at the ranch. However, tonight, she needed some quiet time, so she would head to the diner after she cleaned up.

There, she could clear her mind of one stunning cowboy and his adorable children.

Chapter 5

"Thank you, Grandma," Harlyn shrieked as she wrapped her arms around her Grandma's waist. She accidentally knocked down the overpriced bottles of spring water her parents drank, as if that water didn't come from the same spring the cheaper water came from.

Harlyn hurried to return the bottles to their neat lines and rows that her mother had made the caterers set up.

Turning her attention back to her Grandma, she asked, "Will you put it on me?" The little girl held out the necklace with a key dangling from the end. As it twirled in the air, the sun's reflection blinded Harlyn.

With the sound of footsteps approaching, the older woman clutched the necklace, stuffing it into Harlyn's pocket. She embraced the little girl, whispering, "Never show that to anyone except your Grandpa and me. Your life depends on it."

Harlyn's throat went dry when her mother stared her down like Lady Tremaine did Cinderella. The evilness in that woman's eyes could scare the devil into submission.

A huge, five-tier cake caught Harlyn's attention. Most children love cake, and having that much would impress any nine-year-old, but not Harlyn. Her mother wouldn't let her eat any of it, afraid she'd gain an ounce. Everything with her parents had to be over the top.

Winnie, their housekeeper at the time, rolled the cake out to Harlyn on a stainless steel cart, blocking Harlyn's view of her parents. *Thank you, Winnie.* Her parents intimated their daughter, forcing her to do or say anything they wanted—it was always something that made them look like the dotting parents they most definitely were not.

"You okay, Darlin'?"

Without thinking, Harlyn slid the necklace into Winnie's front pocket, giving her grandparents a wink. Their return smile let Harlyn know that she'd done the right thing.

"Alright, everyone, let's sing Happy Birthday to this beautiful little lady," Winnie had a way of making Harlyn feel special. Her mother should have done that, but no such luck.

Haryln noted that everyone except her parents were singing. It'd been three days since her mother had called her a spoiled brat and locked her in her room. Again, imagine Lady Tremaine locking Cinderella in the tower room.

Sadly, there wasn't a prince waiting to save her. *Not now but someday my prince will rescue me from this dungeon.*

Her parents whispered and looked at her funny. Harlyn's mind wasn't evil enough to even attempt to figure out what they were thinking. Perhaps they could get through the party without any scenes. If they couldn't, Harlyn would pay for it later.

Harlyn felt bile inching up her throat. Her mother stood there with a human being holding an umbrella over her head so the sun didn't mess up her flawless makeup or flatten her heavily sprayed hair that wouldn't move if hurricane-force winds blew through the garden area.

It infuriated Harlyn when her mother referred to hired help as *you or servant.* She'd call them anything that showed her power and dehumanized their existence.

While everyone except for Harlyn and her grandparents ate their cake, her parents made their way gracefully toward them. Their fake laughter and interest in the hundreds of adult guests they'd invited to a child's birthday party hadn't been lost on their daughter. She knew once her parents reached her, something terrible would happen.

"What do I tell them? When they ask?" The same question came every year.

Her grandpa smiled as if they were in a pleasant conversation appropriate for a little girl. "Tell them we got you nothing. We'll set a time to take you shopping this coming week."

Harlyn laughed out loud, catching the attention of the people around her. She hoped to fool her parents into thinking she wasn't having an important conversation.

"Looks like you're having a good time over here," toxic fumes left her mother's mouth like fire from a dragon's.

"You know how Grandpa is, the funniest man I know."

Her dad lowered his voice. "Don't encourage him too much. I've never thought him to be that funny."

"Me, either," her mother replied. "What did they get you for your birthday?"

Harlyn repeated exactly what her grandpa told her, appeasing her mother.

"Perfect. We won't need to worry about needless things cluttering up the mansion."

Harlyn didn't understand why her mother was so mean to Grandpa and Grandma. They were nothing but kind and generous. Grandpa said he'd tell her everything when she got a little older.

Her dad rested his hand on his daughter's shoulder. His fingers dug into her skin, almost making her wince. Almost. She'd learned her lesson before. Never show pain, or more will come. Imagine her surprise the first time that had happened. She'd expected her dad to loosen his grip, knowing he was hurting his daughter—no such luck.

"Oh, look, Dear," his wife Nancy interjected, just as Grandpa stood up. Harlyn knew he was coming to her rescue. "The Jenkles are here. Let's say Hi. Come on, Harlyn."

"No." Everyone's head turned toward Grandpa.

"Excuse me?" Nancy placed her hand on her chest, feigning shock that someone told her *no*. "I think you best let me raise my daughter how I want. I hate to see anything happen to your secure future."

Harlyn had never seen her Grandpa's face so red before. "You listen here—"

"—Keep your voice down, or you will be escorted out."

"Not a problem if that's how you want to play this. I still have a lot of clout over the stockholders. Maybe I should leave right now and enlighten them. They're already suspicious of the rumors floating around."

"Harold, calm down." Esther, his wife, placed a palm on his forearm.

Harlyn didn't know what they were discussing but knew it was important.

"If this ungrateful thing hadn't blabbed lies about us, there wouldn't be any rumors to contend with."

"Let's be real; we know rumors are fake, nontruths," Esther began. "What this beautiful little girl shared were not rumors but the hard, cold facts of what miserable people you two are."

"Don't push me, Esther," Nancy gritted through her teeth. Harlyn couldn't believe how Nancy spoke to her mother.

"Take our time with Harlyn away, and you'll find yourself on the street holding a will-work-for-food cardboard sign," Esther promised. The sweet tone and cherry-red cheeks her grandmother always produced were impressive.

"She can have ten more minutes, and then she must greet Brockton, her future husband."

When Harlyn's parents stalked away, her eyes glassed over. "Husband? I can't marry him. He's a jerk when we're not in front of people. He's like them." The words felt like acid on her tongue.

"Please, can't I go with you guys? Get me out of here."

"I wish you could, Dear. Your mother is trying everything she can to rip you from us, so we have to keep our calm," Esther eyed her husband.

"Sorry."

"As long as we stay one step ahead of her, you will be physically safe. Read the Bible we gave you every night to keep His word in your head and heart. The nasty things they say are lies, just like the devil whispers lies to make us doubt ourselves."

Harlyn fell forward into her grandmother's embrace. Her sweet cinnamon breath made her smile. Halryn loved those hard cinnamon candies. Her grandmother snuck her one every time she could, including today.

"You are special and one-of-a-kind. God has great plans for you." Her grandmother kissed her head.

Chapter 6

He'd promised his kids long ago that as long as Frank and Hazel left the diner open, they could eat dinner there once a week. The food was not bad, but it wasn't as tasty or healthy as Cash and Carolyn's.

The bell above the door jingled, announcing their arrival. Damon noticed Hazel, Myrtle, and Doris in the corner. No doubt scheming about something. No one could ever pin anything on them, but when new blood was in town, these women were sharks engulfing their prey.

Now, that might be a little harsh. All the ladies ever did was set people up with whom they thought would work well together. Fortunately, they'd left Damon alone all these years, and he'd like to keep it that way.

Pointing to the only free table, Damon directed his children that way.

Before they could get there, Myrtle had taken up residency in one of the chairs. "Sorry, guys, but this table is reserved."

Her guileful face told him differently. He only wanted to feed his kids, go home, get them ready for bed, and konk out himself.

As much as he didn't want to make a scene, he challenged her. "I don't believe you." He crossed his arms over his chest. When the lady old enough to be his grandmother smiled and raked her eyes over his chest and arms, he quickly released them and shook his head.

Myrtle pointed at the family just entering the diner. "Them." She stood. "This table is for them." She waved the parents and two children over, welcoming them to the diner. She clearly didn't know the family, probably straggling tourists.

What was she planning?

"Here." Myrtle gripped Damon's arm and gave it an extra squeeze, much to his chagrin. "It wouldn't hurt you to smile every once in a while."

Darlene giggled. "My dad smiles lots."

"I bet he does when playing with you, but he's a first-class grump with everyone else."

"That is true, Dad." Dean began. "You were a little cranky with Harlyn earlier."

Myrtle sucked in a breath. "Is that so? How could anyone be cross with an angel like her?"

Damon used all his power not to roll his eyes. "I apologized."

"Oh, that's great, Dear. I'm sure it's just your emotions rising to the surface."

What!? This woman is too much. Her duo sidekicks were all smiles, shooing their hands toward the back of the diner.

Myrtle led the way, stopping at a private table in the back. "This one would be much better for all of you."

He assumed the table was empty, and by all of you, she meant him and his kids. When he rounded the half-wall, he noticed one of the chairs occupied. He groaned inwardly.

"Harlyn! This is great. We get to eat dinner with you," Darlene cried.

"No, we don't," Damon noted. Harlyn's head snapped to attention like he'd slapped her.

He'd done it now. He should just tattoo *jerk* across his forehead and call it a day.

Her captivating green eyes softened when he said, "I'm not going to push all of us on Harlyn. She obviously wanted to be alone, or she'd be eating at the ranch."

"I don't mind," her response almost immediate, and that was all the invitation his kids needed. Darlene practically sat on Harlyn's lap, and the boys walked around to the other side of the table. That left him with the chair directly across from Harlyn.

How was he supposed to eat dinner, looking at this beautifully, irritating woman throughout his meal?

"It looks like you are all settled. Enjoy your dinner," Myrtle said in a birdsong tone, revealing he'd become her prey.

Harlyn leaned over the table and whispered. "I spent some time with Doris at the salon. Wow, that is all I can say about that. All of them were really pushy tonight, telling me I had to sit here. After hearing about what they did to Willow and the sheriff, they make me nervous."

"With good reason," Damon muttered.

Could he handle two hours locked in a shed with Harlyn? That would depend on whether she was arguing with him. He wasn't ready to admit it, but she was cute when being assertive.

She shrugged and leaned back in her chair, looking irresistible, a temptation Damon needed to resist. They were not a good match. She was mostly sunshine and roses, while he was Oscar—her words, not his.

What had he done to the good Lord above that He would torture Damon so? Pastor Myles had taught him that was not how God worked, and Damon believed it. But sitting across from Harlyn was a sweet torture he never expected or wanted.

"Are you guys into the Marvel movies like Emmanuel?" Harlyn asked the kids while they waited for their dinner to arrive.

"We thought we were Marvel's biggest fans, but as you already know, we were wrong. Emmanuel is the ultimate fan. He knows everything about the character and the actors and actresses who play the characters," Dominic said, sounding discouraged.

"His knowledge is impressive," Harlyn stated, sipping her water. "But his knowledge of something isn't a reflection on you. You can still call yourselves Marvel's biggest fans."

Damon appreciated Harlyn's words. Cheryl had never encouraged the boys. They had to fish for compliments and bless their hearts, they never stopped trying until Cheryl abandoned them. Thankfully, Raddix married a psychologist. The kids may need her services sooner rather than later. *You, too.* A rebel voice pierced through his head, and he shook it free, inhaling deeply.

"Where did you live before the ranch?" Darlene asked Harlyn.

Damon wondered if Harlyn was as comfortable as she claimed to be. Every time one of the kids asked her a question, she sipped her drink before answering.

"All over. That motorhome I parked by my cabin led me wherever I desired."

Darlene spilled her water, and Damon quickly wiped up the liquid and slid his drink toward Darlene, who gulped down half the contents.

"Are you okay?" Damon was concerned by the fear on Harlyn's face. She placed her hand over her stomach as if she had pain radiating through her. *What had happened to her?*

"Yeah, I'm good. Where were we?"

"Your motorhome looks awesome," Dean replied with zest. "Where was your favorite place?"

Harlyn thought for a minute. "I liked the Grand Canyon, but the Grand Tetons were nice, and so was Alcatraz."

Dean, the oldest at almost thirteen, piped up, "That place gives me the creeps."

"Why?" Darlene asked.

Damon pinned his eldest with a stern look. "Don't. She'll have night-mares."

This was yet another reason why Damon has considered talking to Lily about Darlene. She still hadn't outgrown nightmares, and she always wanted to crawl into bed with Damon at night, but he refused. Bringing her back to her room, he sat with her until she fell asleep, then stumbled back to his bed.

Appreciation filled Damon when Harlyn changed the subject.

"When I was a kid, I spent every summer and sometimes parts of the year at a farm my family owned in Florida. There were horses there. I had some training, like staying on a tame horse and living to tell about it. They always intimidated me."

"My dad has a Gold Buckle. He won it when I was two," Darlene inter-rupted.

Darlene always bragged about him. Usually, he liked it, but right now, he felt heat creep into his neck. "Don't interrupt, Sweetheart."

"Impressive," Harlyn's eyes locked with his.

Now, the heat rose into his face. What did her *impressive* mean? Was it meant in a buckle bunny kind of way or a genuine, you've got a talent, and it's appreciated? Harlyn never struck him as the buckle bunny type, so maybe she was amazed.

"Dad, are you okay?" Dominic asked.

"I'm good; it's just hot in here. Now let Harlyn finish her story."

"I'm not hot. Are you hot, Dean?"

"Nope." He let the *p* pop, telling Damon his boys knew what was happening to their old man. Leave it to the tween and teen to make his father even more uncomfortable than he already was.

"Anyway," Harlyn continued. "I have a funny story. I was at a campground in Texas. I'd brought my flippers and goggles to see the lake creatures. I'd made friends with some of the other guests, and we decided to relax on a rectangular, wooden raft, you know, to catch a little bit of sun."

Harlyn took a sip of her water before she continued. Damon's heart swelled, watching his kids hang on Harlyn's every word.

"After who knows how long, we decided to snorkel." Harlyn squirmed in her seat, and then the kids followed suit. Damon had to admit that he couldn't wait to discover what happened.

"I slid my foot in my flipper. Something started hopping on the tips of my toes. I kicked that baby off. It flew a couple of feet in the air. On its way down, a frog ejected from the flipper."

"What happened next?" Dean rushed to ask.

"Unfortunately, it continued to hop on my leg, then my stomach. The more I backed up and screamed, the more it hopped. That was until . . ."

Damon moved his hand in a circular motion, urging her to finish the story.

"Her cheeks flushed. Man, was she cute.

"I leaned too close to the metal ladder, and my bathing suit bottom snagged on the end of a screw or the bolt, I don't know. I lost my balance and fell in the water."

Damon bit his cheek to keep from laughing. Harlyn was unique. Cheryl had never laughed when Damon teased her. In fact, she'd rather rip her pretty painted nails off than tell a story that would make her look bad.

Dominic's low voice spoke first. "That's rough."

"Epic," Dean followed next.

"Were you okay?" Darlene wondered aloud.

Harlyn nodded. "Yeah, besides a mad incision down my thigh and a major rip in my suit, forcing me to wrap my towel around my waist quickly and call it a day."

Damon wished their food had arrived. He needed something to focus on besides Harlyn's thigh and ripped bathing suit. His mind shouldn't be wondering how badly her suit had been torn, but it was.

"You're so cool. Our mom never told stories about herself if they made her look bad," Dean declared. Damon nodded in agreement, happy he wasn't the only one thinking that.

"When we get back to the ranch, will you go through my bedtime routine with me?" Darlene asked innocently.

Damon held his breath, waiting for Harlyn's response.

Her jaw dropped slightly, but she recovered it quickly. "Sure, as long as it's okay with your dad."

She didn't just do that. *If I say no, I'll be the bad guy.* "That sounds like an excellent plan." Perhaps he had too much enthusiasm because he had four sets of eyes staring him down as if he were from outer space.

Damon welcomed more time with Harlyn so he could get to know her better since she spent so much time with his kids. *Sure, that's the reason. You like her, just admit it!*

Chapter 7

Harlyn's grandmother died without notice. Harold and Esther had taken Harlyn to pick out a dress for an upcoming party at her parent's mansion. Harlyn had a closet full of dresses; many still had the tags on, but her mother insisted she get a new one.

Harlyn remembered the moment vividly. "Sure, I'll get a new dress. Under one condition," she folded her arms, looking past her mother. "Grandpa and Grandma take me to get it."

A staring showdown ensued. Had she pushed her mother too far? Minutes, probably more like seconds, ticked by.

"If that's what she wants, Nancy, let her have dinner with her grandparents."

Shock filled her gut. Her dad just stood up to her mother.

"Fine. We'll have dinner with them first, and then you get the dress."

An inner smile lit up Harlyn's chest. She finally beat her mother at her own game. "Really? Your parents can take me?" Harlyn clarified, concerned with how easy this was.

"Yes!" Irritation pricked Nancy's voice as she strode away. "Get ready. Dinner will be served when they arrive." Her mother left her, presumably to call her grandparents.

Harlyn sat ramrod straight, the expectation, at the dining table. She loathed the lavender frilly dress her mother made her wear but endured it to spend time with Harold and Esther.

Emma, the newest and youngest member of the mansion's staff, refilled everyone's water glasses. While reaching across the table, a big no-no in Nancy's mind, the young girl knocked over Esther's glass, cracking it when it connected with her grandmother's plate. Nancy cursed at Emma and told her to take the glass and be gone.

"Here, Esther, have my water," Nancy said, sliding the glass toward her mother. Fortunately, the rest of the dinner was uneventful—just how Harlyn liked it.

Finally, Harlyn was with her grandparents at the dress boutique, lazily looking through her options, feigning indecisiveness so she could spend more time with them. Then, her grandma complained of not feeling well. They made a quick purchase, and as they dropped Harlyn off at the mansion, kissing her goodnight, her grandma said, "No matter what anyone says, know that I love you very much."

She took it at face value then, not realizing that would be the last time she'd see Esther alive.

Nancy lacked compassion even when her mother died. "Stop your whining," Nancy barked at her one and only child. "Your grandmother wouldn't want you to waste tears on her."

Harlyn wouldn't argue with Lady Tremaine's twin sister—that's something her grandmother wouldn't want.

"Crying shows weakness," Nancy said absentmindedly as she strode through the hallway.

Just leave me alone, she screamed inside her head, hoping God would make her mother do it without her having to say anything and suffer.

"You can come out when you have control of yourself." *Perfect. I'll never have control of myself, so I never have to leave this room until I'm ready to go for good.*

Before shutting the door, Harlyn heard Winnie, their house manager. "Mrs. Summers, Brockton is here to see Harlyn."

Harlyn snapped, "No, thank you. He's the last person I want to see."

Her mother rushed toward her, got within an inch of her face, and gritted through her teeth, "Don't you dare mess this deal up for your father and me. You will marry that boy someday, so you might as well get used to him now."

Deal? Fear trickled down her spine. Harlyn nodded her head, hoping the good Lord would protect her from having to marry the likes of Brockton Jenkles III.

Running her palm down her dress, Nancy pulled her shoulders back. With a low, controlled tone, she addressed Winnie. "She's got a splitting headache, so if she's not herself, let me know, and I'll see if I can give her something to take care of it." Nancy shot daggers at her daughter.

Harlyn knew what that meant. Her throat clogged briefly before she responded, "I'll be just fine, Mother," disdain dripped from Harlyn's lips as she complied and Brockton entered her room.

"I thought so." Nancy shut the door, latching it with a clicking sound.

"What was that about?" Brockton sounded genuinely interested, but she'd learned by now that he was just a mole carrying information back to the powers that be.

Harlyn would never tell another soul, especially Brockton, how Winnie snuck her a letter from her Grandpa. She stashed it under her mattress for now. Grandpa was convinced that Nancy laced Grandma's water with something lethal. She wouldn't be surprised if Nancy made Emma spill Esther's drink so she could give her the infected water.

"I'm not sure." Lies. All lies. *Please forgive me, Father.* She refused to tell Brockton anything she didn't want repeated.

"You'll have to trust me at some point." Brockton ran his knuckle across her cheek, making her wince. Though he was only fifteen, Brockton acted more like an adult, trying to seduce her. "What's your problem?"

"My grandmother just died, and you're making me feel uncomfortable."

"I'm trying to protect you, show you I'm there for you, Brockton countered.

Harlyn let out a big puff of air. "Well, you're going about it all wrong."

At one time, Brockton had been kind and fun to hang out with, but for the last six years, he'd been boring, demanding, and obnoxious. Things she once found attractive, like his dark brown eyes, now reminded her of beady balls of evilness waiting to attack unsuspecting prey. Sadly, she seemed to be the prey.

He sat next to her, placing his hand on her knee. "I'm here for you." She nodded and pulled her leg away, his hand dropping to the side of the bed.

Meanwhile, her heart raced, wanting to finish reading her letter. She laughed inwardly, knowing that her future awaited her in that letter, resting under the heaviness of that mat while the boy beside her was the only familiarity she had with her expected future, one that her grandparents were adamant she needed to escape. But how?

"Look, I don't like this any more than you do, but we are set to be engaged at nineteen, married at twenty, and living happily ever after. I will not let you mess with those plans. I don't expect you to stay faithful to me; I certainly won't you."

Wait. What?! Slam on the brakes!

Who is this person? Brockton had become worse than she thought. *Had her parents gotten to him? What did they promise him? Obviously, it's something big.* Harlyn had news for all of them. She wouldn't marry anyone unless it were for love. Ever!

Chapter 8

Harlyn noted the pictures of the kids on the wall as she traversed the hallway in Damon's living space. This was one of the bigger cabins on the ranch. It had three bedrooms, a living room, and a kitchen. Dominic and Dean didn't seem to mind sharing a room. While reading to Darlene, she admitted that being the only girl had its advantages.

"I get my own room." She twirled around the bright room. Darlene's room revealed a lot about her. The small shelf crowded with books matched her avid desire for learning. Her lavender-painted walls with horse stickers and flowers spoke to her tender heart.

"And there's all these hunky men around to protect me." The girl's words caught Harlyn by surprise.

"What!? One of those men is your dad, you know?" *Darlene wasn't old enough to notice flushed cheeks, was she?*

"So you do find him hunky. Dean was right." Darlene put a finger to her chin and acted like she was conjuring up a plan. One that would probably embarrass Harlyn more than the frog incident.

Harlyn couldn't believe Damon's children were discussing whether or not she thought their dad was a hunk. *I wonder if they asked Damon what he felt about me.* Oh, wow, Harlyn should not be concerned about that. They argued too much over silly things. She and Damon were lucky to pass for civil during work hours; anything beyond that would be asking for trouble.

"All I'm saying is you shouldn't be talking about the men in such an adult way." Good save, or so she hoped so.

"Miss Katy said with all these cowboys, the ranch is the safest place to live." Darlene smiled, pulling the covers up to her neck.

From her lips to God's ears.

"I bet my dad's listening," she whispered in Harlyn's ear when they heard a scuffle outside her door.

"Yeah, my dad is the hunkiest. He's strong and nice." Unable to finish, Darlene started giggling.

"Good night, Darlene. Keep yourself out of trouble." Harlyn reached the door and turned back when the little girl spoke.

"Good night, Harlyn. Thank you."

Harlyn's heart melted like a snowcone on a midsummer's day in Florida. Getting to know Darlene made Harlyn want children even more.

When she opened the door, Harlyn caught Damon's piercing cocoa eyes for a nanosecond. His strong jaw and smug smile drew her in—he'd heard the entire conversation. She could feel the heat in her cheeks; hopefully, he couldn't see it.

Damon barely gave her any room to close the door. Once it was shut, they were inches apart. He extended his hand toward the hallway.

Why had that simple gesture sent shots of awareness through her body? His nearness had her mind swirling and her pulse racing, a foreign feeling for her. He was having her walk down the hallway first—probably so he could shove her out the door at the first chance.

Harlyn spun on her heels in the living room, her palms caught on his solid chest. He *was* even closer than she thought. Her brain kept telling her to remove her hands—they would not listen.

Her eyes finally drifted from his chest to meet his eyes. What a mistake!

Those brown-as-polished mahogany beauties spoke to her this evening with a playfulness she never expected from this man—he had challenged her every step of the way, and now he was sending her a different message.

Her breath hitched being this close to him.

Only then did she notice his hands resting on her hips. *Had they been there the whole time, or did he see her inability to remove her hands from his solid chest as an invitation?*

She opted for a quick escape. Begrudgingly, she let her hands fall. "I-I'm sorry," she stuttered and stepped back, his hands thumping off his upper thighs.

Real smooth, Har.

He ran his hand through his hair. "Would you like some coffee or something? If we have to work together, we should know each other better."

"If that means you'll stop being so broody with me, then sure, I'd love some," she managed to say without making a fool of herself.

Ten minutes later, they sat next to each other on the couch, sipping their coffee.

"Tell me about your ex-wife," Harlyn spoke up.

He choked on his drink, some dribbling back into his cup. "What do you want to know?"

"What'd she look like? How long were you together? What did you love about her; things like that."

"Well, there's a picture of her over on the wall. It was taken about six months before she left. Darlene was only two. We'd been together since our senior year in high school when her family moved into town."

"Are you from Montana?"

"No, southeast Wyoming. My parents owned a ranch."

Harlyn set her empty cup on the table and rose to view the family picture on the wall. She wasn't sure if seeing Cheryl was a good idea. She imagined the woman as a pretty blonde with voluptuous curves everywhere, and she was correct. Harlyn's polar opposite.

What did that matter? It shouldn't, but Harlyn's family had always compared her to others, so why wouldn't she?

She studied the picture. Damon's big smile revealed a happily married man. Cheryl's smile appeared plastered on, like she'd rather be elsewhere, and then the kids were just adorable. Dominic with his front teeth missing. *Aw!*

"I can see what you loved about her, so no need to answer that question," she said dryly.

Fortunately, he'd just finished his coffee but coughed the same. "Wow, so you think I'm a pretty superficial guy, only dating a woman for her looks?"

She whipped around. "No, I didn't mean that. I was just noting her beautiful features."

"Yeah, they aren't so beautiful when you get to know her on the inside," Damon said dryly.

Harlyn noted the disdain in his voice.

When Harlyn returned to the couch, she tucked her feet behind her and rested her head in her hand propped on the back of the couch. Damon pulled one leg onto the couch.

"I'm sorry. Let's move away from the ex-wife topic and tell me more about how you grew up."

"Nice try," he flashed her a devilish smile. "It's my turn."

"Okay, shoot."

"Tell me about your exes?"

Did his eager tone mean he was interested? Probably not. It didn't matter anyway. She'd never been able to stay in one place long enough to make lasting relationships. Would that ever change?

If she could, this would be the place to do it. Harlyn felt at ease on the ranch. Everyone here was trustworthy.

"I'm not sure you want to hear this," Harlyn whispered.

"Come on. I told you—"

"—Nothing," she interrupted. Damon seemed adamant to keep his feelings to himself.

"You don't have to tell me if you don't want to, but I am a good listener. Besides. I need the listening practice for when Darlene starts dating."

"I wasn't allowed to date, ever, Harlyn began. "The power couple, Bill and Nancy Summers, AKA my parents. started off humbly but soon became considered legendary in the financial world; I refer to them as demons."

She picked her cup back up, wishing she still had something to drink, but maybe holding it would help her focus.

"From a very early age, I was told who I'd marry—Brockton Jenkles III. Our parents were friends, as much as elitists can have friends. They spent their time together at the country club, or we dined at each other's mansions. Real boring stuff."

"Sounds fun."

She liked Damon's sarcasm.

"When I turned nineteen, I'd run out of time." Harlyn paused when Damon sat up straighter."

"Brockton proposed like our parents forced him to do. I accepted in the moment, knowing what would happen if I didn't."

"What?"

"That's another story for a different day."

She gripped her cup even more and subconsciously brought the mug to her lips for a sip. Damon must have known it was empty. He removed the mug from her hand, replacing it with the throw pillow from behind him. Their fingers brushed against each other, sending a jolt of energy through her.

"Thank you." She hugged it to her chest. "As we walked in the garden, he told me we'd get married that weekend; something about having a wife to go on some married couples-only event with his company."

She shivered, recalling that that night. "It wasn't his words; it was how he said them. The final indignity was when he said I had to give up my photography to have babies and be the picture-perfect wife." She made a gagging sound.

"You win. No more talking about exes for now," Damon declared, his fist in tight balls.

The way his corded muscles flexed was a pleasant distraction that had heat rising in Harlyn's chest.

She brought her cup to the sink and stared out the window into the black night, wondering if she was brave enough to venture out to her own cabin.

Damon approached from behind, startling her. "I'm sorry." He placed a hand on her shoulder, sending an electric current down the length of her arm. She wasn't sure what he was apologizing for but assumed it was for jumping her. "Let me walk you to your door. You never know what animals will greet you at night."

"What about the kids?" She really appreciated his chivalry but refused to put his kids in danger. She'd been on her own for a while now and would have to continue relying on herself.

"I'm not spending the night," he blurted out. The pink hue in his cheeks made Harlyn giggle.

"No need to be embarrassed. I know what you meant."

Damon ran his hand through his hair again, making her fingers jealous.

"Do you always call it as you see it?"

"Yup. No point in hiding things. Our actions reveal the truth anyway."

Chapter 9

Harlyn: Sixteen-Years-Old

Despite her spacious bedroom, which only had a princess bed, a long eight-drawer bureau, and a vanity, Harlyn felt claustrophobic. Her private bathroom was larger than most people's primary bathroom. Her favorite place was her balcony. From there, she took pictures of the grounds and read her Bible.

She sat there now, still in disbelief. After telling everyone who could help her about her parents' corrupt actions, no one listened. Even the most recent bruises weren't enough for others to step in. Instead, her parents sent her to her room, and all they gave Harlyn was a drink—one she *accidentally* spilled off the balcony. That was two days ago. Fortunately, she had a secret stash of crackers.

On the second day of her lockdown, Winnie smuggled in another letter from her grandpa.

> *Harlyn, My Darling Granddaughter,*
>
> *You are nearing your freedom. Remember these two things. It's nothing new, I just don't want you to forget.*
>
> *1.) Never drink or eat anything your parents give you. Accidentally spill it or dump it down the drain.*
>
> *2) Never, **ever** marry Brockton.*

It would be over her dead body she marry Brockton. He always said, "*That can be arranged,*" whenever she told him such. The stiffness in his jaw and hatred oozing from his eyes told her he meant it. But so did she. Harlyn knew she would be with Jesus when she died, so Harlyn didn't see a problem with that potential outcome.

Her eyes refocused on the letter, finding the spot she'd left off.

> *There are things I cannot tell you by law, but you will find out soon enough. I have everything you need for your freedom. When the time is right, I will give it all to you. Your mother may keep us apart right now, but justice will prevail. Trust me, I'm working on it.*
>
> *Love you – Grandpa*

Harlyn put the letter down. She'd memorize it tonight and get rid of it. She never cried anymore. Her parents always found out and tried to toughen her up. The final straw for Harlyn was the puppy. Her parents bought her a puppy, and when they wanted her to comply, they tortured the sweetie.

Despite her efforts to *fall in line,* Harlyn slipped one day (because the line was constantly moving), and she never saw her puppy again.

A knock at her door made her jump. She quickly jammed the letter inside the book and slammed it shut, stuffing it under the bed just as her father walked in.

"I'm heading out of town for a couple of weeks for work. Please just do what your mother says so you stay safe while I'm gone."

In the last couple of months, ever since Nancy had deemed Harlyn's grandpa mentally unfit to make decisions and hadn't let him come around, her dad had changed. He no longer tried to intimate Harlyn or hurt her. In fact, he'd started sneaking things to Harlyn. *Is he a wolf in sheep's clothing or the Trojan Horse?* The Bible says when things don't seem right, they probably aren't.

Her dad was moving around the room, placing clothing over picture frames and wall art. Harlyn was tempted to ask what he was doing. Even though he'd been more approachable—when her mother wasn't around—she still didn't trust him. Harlyn's heart cringed at the thought.

He motioned to the balcony, where Harlyn joined him. Every minute detail throughout the house extended to the outside balcony that no one except for Harlyn would see. The porcelain tiled floor extended five feet past the door. The smooth, glass-like feeling under her feet chilled her entire body. The bright white cylinder-shaped pillars had intricate lines the length of each column. The square base at the bottom of each massive pole sported a design representing her mother's family. Nancy had never explained the meaning, and Harlyn didn't care to know anymore. Anything to do with her mother's family, except her Grandpa, of course,

Harlyn didn't want anything to do with it. Her dad gripped the black rod iron railing. Staring out at the perfectly manicured lawn, pool area, and one section of the lazy river that circled the entire estate, he let out a breath and finally spoke.

"I just covered all the cameras in your room. This balcony is the only safe place. Your mother said she was upgrading the camera system with sound, but I don't know if she'd done that or not. Be very careful."

Harlyn had wondered about her dad's one-eighty. He'd been taking more work trips and avoiding Nancy when he was home. Something was very wrong besides the obvious.

"What game are you playing now?" Harlyn couldn't help herself.

"No game. This situation is bigger than even I knew."

"What does that mean?"

Her dad shook his head. "I can't tell you. You must listen to your Grandfather. Things are about to hit the fan. Do not believe anything Brockton or his parents have to say. Obviously, don't listen to your mother either. She is taking me to the airport now. Expect her back in forty-five minutes. Winnie has a surprise for you. Stay safe."

Bill kissed her forehead and walked back into her room, leaving Harlyn flabbergasted on the balcony.

It wasn't ten minutes later when she saw her parents leave the estate in her mother's Royal Royce, Hector driving them around like Morgan Freeman's character in Driving Miss Daisy. Hector was just as nice as the actor's character, but his pleasantries were saved for Winnie.

Harlyn thought they were cute when she caught them cuddling. A pain ached in her chest, feeling hopeless. Would she ever find a guy to cuddle? One who wasn't trying to get something out of her?

Five minutes later, another knock came at her door.

"Come in."

Harlyn hurdled over her bed when her grandpa strolled in. She hadn't seen him alone in three months. Her arms, like a vice grip clutched around his waist.

"You only have thirty minutes then Harold has to go." Winnie ran a tight ship so no one got caught. Harlyn appreciated her.

"Something big is about to go down. My attorneys and private investigators are ready and prepared, keeping me a few steps ahead of your mother."

Her grandpa was as lucid as she was. Would Harlyn make it another couple of years under this roof?

Her mother was Thanos, Venom, and Magneto, all wrapped into one. *Good grief.* One day, she'll have to answer for her actions.

"Why can't I know what's going on?"

"It puts you in more danger." He led her to the edge of her bed, where they slowly descended but remained embraced. "What I can tell you is that my attorney and private investigator are tracking every transaction and business meeting happening. My money has been secured."

The eerie feeling holding her hostage irritated Harlyn. What was it that her grandpa wasn't telling her in the name of safety? Was he in danger? His welfare was just as important.

"This extends to Brockton and his parents as well." Harold broke into her thoughts. "From what my P.I. told me, they are not as friendly as they'd like everyone to believe, and they have corrupted Brockton with ultimatums and deals that a snake like him will never pass up. Stay far away. I am going to confront your mother when she returns. I have enough on her that she will no longer keep us apart. I'm still working on taking her down completely. I believe we'll find it."

Harlyn smiled. "Psalm 27:14 tells us to *Wait on the LORD; Be of good courage, And He shall strengthen your heart; Wait, I say, on the LORD!*"

"Good Girl. *All good things come from God.*" Harold shared his own Bible quote.

Chapter 10

The sun spoke to Damon this morning, giving him the extra motivation to focus on training Meadow. His mind was consumed with the newest member of Big L' Ranch.

From the moment Damon met Harlyn, as he sat perched on the collapsable bench in the dunk tank at the End of Summer Festival, his interest had been piqued.

He'd tried to ignore the prickling in his chest and the adrenaline flowing through his veins whenever she was around. Knowing that he couldn't keep Cheryl happy, why would he bother trying with someone else?

After hearing about Harlyn's past, Damon was ready to throttle that Brockton dude and her parents. He'd spent years feeling sorry for himself, like Cheryl was the end all be all. Yet, Harlyn's life seemed akin to living on

The Rock. Dean's mention of it at dinner seemed random until now. Poor Harlyn.

"At least she's safe here," Quinton let out a slow breath, shock registering on his face after hearing Damon's report.

"Did she say it was okay to tell us?" Amelia questioned as she helped prep the other horses for Damon.

Damon paused. Why were women so difficult? He wasn't concerned about upsetting Harlyn by telling Amelia and Quinton. His only goal was to keep her safe.

"No."

"Maybe you should let her come to us on her own if she's concerned," Amelia suggested.

Damon ran his hand over his face, frustration eating at his insides.

Though Damon didn't know Harlyn well, he surmised that she wouldn't like them making a big deal about her past, but people needed to know if she needed protection.

Swallowing, he watched Harlyn enter the barn and move toward the trio.

"Hey, Darlene wants me to take pics of her and the kids right now. Is that okay, or should I ask every parent?"

"As long as you're doing it for the kids and not releasing them anywhere, I know all the parents would be fine with that," Amelia answered.

Damon found her to be a reputable photographer who'd already won over his kids' hearts. "I'd love a picture of my three kiddos without their mom if you wouldn't mind doing that."

"Sure, any background requests?" The smile on her face did funny things to his chest. *Ignore that. She's only excited about taking photos.* He deflated on the inside, knowing her bright sunshine would never be attracted to the perpetual cloud hanging over him.

"Whatever you think looks good."

Her rosy pink cheeks caught his attention. Without notice, his renegade eyes roamed over her smooth-looking lips and slightly curvy hips where his hands recently rested . . . *Focus!* He cleared his throat, hoping no one was paying him any mind.

"How's everything going for you, Harlyn?" Amelia inquired.

"I love it here. God works miracles. Thank you for allowing me this opportunity. I don't know where I'd be without it."

Damon and Harlyn shared a look. Any reluctance on Damon's part about being around her had nothing to do with her work ethic or knowledge of cultivating and growing crops. Rather, he didn't want her in danger; her stubbornness made it challenging.

He'd already told Jeff, but his response wasn't helpful. "The challenging ones are the most fun to chase."

As if. Damon wasn't about to chase anyone. He wouldn't stand by and let someone harm this woman, either.

Did Jeff know something he didn't? Could Damon bring another woman into their lives? Cheryl had left all of them. She blamed Damon, accusing him of choosing his career over her, thus ripping the family apart.

That had been eight years ago. Darlene, his youngest, had only been two when Cheryl left. Her manipulation didn't fool Damon. She didn't like the country and used him as a patsy to leave.

After his last competition, she thought Damon would quit the sport and leave the ranch. Eventually, grief pushed him to retire, but he would never leave Big L' Ranch.

"It appears that you two are working well together. Are there any issues or concerns you're having, either of you?" Amelia questioned as she finished up her chore..

Issue?

Haryln's too sweet and attractive. A major distraction, pushing me to my limits.

"Damon?" Quinton pulled him back into the conversation. "It looks like you have something to say." The corner of his lip twitched.

I'll get him for this.

"No, Quinton. I'm good." Damon crossed his arms over his chest.

"Harlyn, have you decided whether you'll stay on for the winter yet?" Amelia asked.

Leaving? Why would she leave? Was his arguing with her getting on her nerves? *Maybe you should stop acting like a teenage boy and be straightforward with her.*

"I'm quite positive I will, but can I have the week to make my final decision?"

"Sure," Amelia said, wiping her hands on her jeans.

Damon could tell by the mischievous look on Quinton's face that he'd read Damon's mind or at least seen the distress of her leaving written all over his face. Quinton knew Damon's problem was with being around Harlyn Summers, the bombshell, had nothing to do with Harlyn, the agricultural specialist or photographer.

This kind-hearted, attractive woman interfered with his ability to focus on his job. The last thing he needed was to get into the corral with a wild stang and get stomped to smithereens because she'd taken up permanent residency in his mind.

Yep, this was his problem, and the smiling fool in front of him wouldn't help. All those times he razzed Quinton about having the hots for Amelia the second she opened the door for his interview were coming back to haunt him.

"Hey, Dad! Dean came barreling into the barn. "Can we use your horses for our pictures?"

"Sure." He stuffed the end of the pitchfork into the hay barrel.

"I think that's a great idea. Staring at Cheryl day in and day out can't be healthy for any of you," Quinton offered his opinion.

"Isn't Lily's the psychologist?" His eyes glared at his boss, trying to stop him from whatever game he was playing.

"Dad," Dean interrupted the playful tension building between the men. "Darlene wants Harlyn to be in at least one picture with us."

An awkward silence fell over the barn. Damon clenched his fist, wishing to knock the smirk off Quinton's face. He wouldn't put Harlyn in a difficult situation like that. Both of their pasts were too intense for them to move on.

Right?

Just then, they locked eyes. Her silky blonde hair rested against the front of her shoulder, and her full, pouty lips called his name. Little beads of sweat started forming on his brow. *Keep it together.*

Damon cleared his throat, allowing him to respond. "We'll see how it goes."

"Are we done here?" Quinton asked with a grin.

"Yep," Damon replied as Dean disappeared, and Quinton laced his fingers with his wife's, guiding her toward the door.

"Can you wait a minute?" Harlyn called out.

"I don't know where to start," Harlyn said somberly.

His anticipation revved up as she fiddled with her fingers. If she had a drink, she'd probably drown her insides before even speaking. His need to pull her into his chest and calm her emotions flooded his body.

"It's okay, Harlyn. These guys are safe people," I tried to assure her.

"I really want to stay on permanently, but I don't think that's best. I should leave now," she blurted.

"Why?" Amelia asked, her tone concerned.

Hopefully, he hadn't chased her off, too. It hadn't even been twenty-four hours since he'd walked her home. He hadn't even tried to kiss her, though every nerve ending had urged him to do so.

Harlyn had seemed, as Dean would say, *chill*. Her body language, or so he thought, had said, *kiss me*, but he refrained—playing it safe, watching her enter her cabin. He left when he heard the deadbolt latch.

She remained quiet for a long while. Had she left out parts of the story last night that she hadn't wanted him to know? He didn't want to imagine whatever else she'd endured before arriving at the ranch.

Harlyn let out a hard breath.

"Long story short, I was supposed to marry someone but ran away. He keeps finding me, so I keep moving. I received an email from Brockton. He said, and I quote, "You can't hide out in Haven Ridge any longer. I'm coming to get what is mine. That's you!"

Quinton was the first to speak. "You're not going anywhere."

Everyone snapped their heads toward him.

"His guy sounds dangerous, and there won't be any place safer than this ranch."

"Agreed." Amelia and Damon said in unison.

Harlyn shook her head. "I will not have others putting themselves in danger for me. More importantly, I don't want anything to happen to any of the kids."

Something wasn't settling well with Damon. How did they know where she was?

"Do you have your location on?"

"Not unless it was by accident. I lived on burner phones until that became obnoxious and went phoneless. It wasn't until I released all my bodyguards that I got my phone. I never enabled my location." She pulled up the settings app and revealed to the group that her location was off.

"Well, they're finding you somehow." Damon gave her a stern look. "But I know one thing. They can't have you."

Harlyn Summers was staying right here at Big L' Ranch.

Chapter 11

The promise ring Brockton placed on her finger five hundred twenty-seven days ago felt like a noose strangling the life out of her. As she lay in her bed with her ankles crossed, she tried to daydream about her future, but his incessant texting drove her insane.

Harlyn would scream if she received one more text asking questions that didn't matter to her.

What type of ring do you see yourself wearing?

One that someone else gives me.

Harlyn erased that before she accidentally sent it. She was too close to freedom to botch it now. She'd spent all day writing a letter to her parents, expressing her feelings—no-holds-barred style.

Another text pinged on her phone.

> **Are you opposed to a very short engagement? I want to get to the benefits of marriage.**

Eww! Dear God, please help me. She couldn't even fathom how to respond besides yelling, *"No! Never. Over my dead body."* Scratch the last part. She wouldn't remind him of his options.

Harlyn had been praying for years this day would come. Tomorrow, she'd turned eighteen, and she could fly the coop. The last week, she'd been fasting and reading her Bible. No answers seemed to pop out at her. Yes, she expected something—answers to where she'd go or how she'd escape. Fortunately, God had given her great insight and the ability to deflect the conversation whenever Brockton brought up marriage before. Now, however, he was like an assiduous bulldog, scaring Harlyn into a corner.

> **Don't ignore me.**

Ugh! He was relentless. He turned everything into a battle. Should she respond?

No! She would not cower now. Her freedom was mere hours away. She wasn't sure of the specifics yet, but she knew Brockton, his parents, and her parents were not in her future. Right now, her parents were off galavanting at a party for the rich and tasteless, as Harlyn coined them. *So much for my father's one-eighty. More than ever, he acted like her mother's lackey.*

Harlyn slid to the edge of her bed, letting her feet dangle. Based on her watch, Grandpa should be there to visit any moment. It was like she blinked, and he walked through her door. His worried, pursed lips had her on her feet.

"What's wrong?"

Could her freedom be this close yet still out of reach? She'd had enough. Harlyn couldn't wait any longer. *Be still* rang through her head, causing her anger to spike. *Sorry, Lord. I don't know how much longer I can be still. I've been waiting for You. Please give me some answers.*

One of the many things she loved about Grandpa was that he never beat around the bush. "I'm dying."

Her knees buckled. This was nowhere near what she'd been thinking. *I think you gave me the wrong answer, God.* She knew he hadn't. God never made mistakes. Her erratic breathing picked up the pace.

"Here, sit." Her grandpa navigated her back to her bed and slowly lowered her down. Sitting next to her, he explained that he'd been diagnosed with liver cancer. The projected life expectancy for that was not good, but she served a powerful God, and Grandpa wouldn't stay on Earth one minute longer than God wanted, nor would he head to Heaven one minute earlier.

For as long as she could remember, Harlyn had the family secrets and abuse weighing her down. She'd been without her grandmother for years, and now, without seeing her Grandpa as often as she'd like, Harlyn's shoulders sagged.

Despite the morbid news, the sun would shine permanently on her heart the nanosecond she left this awful mansion. It'd only taken eighteen years, but finally, hope rang through her soul. She would escape. Her grandparents' efforts would not go by the wayside.

"I purchased a motorhome under the pretense of me leaving, traveling around the country to live out my last days."

Tears filled her eyes to their brim. "Don't talk like that." She sunk her head into his shoulder. The warmth of his arm on her shoulder was the most protected she'd ever felt.

"Of course, your mother was thrilled with that idea."

"I overheard her talking to my father the other night. She argued that life would be better once her dad died." Grandpa's rockhard jaw didn't budge, but his eyes drooped slightly. *How could she say that about Grandpa? Please, Lord, never let me be as vile as her.*

"In truth, it is for you. "I'll make my traveling believable, but, Buttercup, just know it's yours. Great things are coming your way."

The brave facade of courage and confidence that Harlyn had built for years was starting to break down into fear and doubt. What if her mother caught her? Her father only looked out for himself. Then, there was Brockton. What to say about him? Yesterday, he yelled at her when she didn't give him a straight answer about what type of cake she wanted at the reception. *Good, golly, what do I care? I won't be there!* His parents hadn't spoken with hers in what seemed like forever. Were they fighting? Harlyn rarely paid attention to their gatherings, but something just felt off.

I don't care. I'm going to leave and never see these people again.

An abrupt knock on her bedroom door almost took it off its hinges. Harlyn jumped a foot off her bed.

All out of breath, Winnie's chest heaved as she leaned onto the door knob. "Brockton . . . is . . . heading this . . . way."

Harlyn rocketed off her bed. "He's probably mad because I didn't respond to his text."

He slowly stood. "I'm not going too far then. That slimy coward wouldn't dare do anything with me around."

"But won't Mother keep making life difficult for you?"

He winked at her. "I'm preparing to leave, finish off my dying days. She sees this as a blessing, I'm sure. She's not stupid. Nancy knows how to bide her time."

Harold's cell phone pinged with a text. He pulled it from his pocket. Handing it to Harlyn. "Will you read it, please? I don't have my glasses."

Wided-eyed and jittery, Harlyn choked, "Um . . . we have a bigger problem than Brockton coming here." Her arms fell with a thump against the front of her quads, "I'm not going anywhere."

Chapter 12

C an you say *sexy?*

Harlyn had been repulsed when Brockton got possessive and ordered her around.

Last week, when Damon said that neither Brockton nor her parents could have her and that she would stay at the ranch, her heart melted into a puddle.

This afternoon, she and Katy traveled an hour to Beaverhead, where Harlyn picked up the picture she'd taken of Damon and the kids on their horses.

Recollection of that day came rushing back to her. After the pictures, they played. Damon twirled Darlene around whenever he caught her during their tag game. He wrestled with the boys while Darlene acted as the ref, getting down on her belly and making sure the person's shoulders remained grounded. Her three count was fast as Meadow racing in the field when her brothers had Damon pinned, but whenever Damon pinned the boys, Darlene forgot to play referee.

As she watched them, she experienced external happiness for the first time in her life. She'd always known true joy came from within, but now, being part of the Richards clan felt like the center of a chocolate chip cookie right out of the oven—warm and gooey. Despite her past, she'd always trusted God and the Holy Spirit to guide her way. *Thank you, Lord, for leading me here.*

When Darlene begged Harlyn to help the three kids pin their dad, she joined in the fun. Quickly, she realized how strong Damon was—holding off the two youngest with one arm, Dean and Harlyn attacked him on his right. When they all fell in a heap, the kids rolled out of the way, leaving Harlyn wrapped in Damon's arms.

"Well, hello there," his husky voice reverberated through her body.

The kids, more like little masterminds, had duped her. All was forgiven as he gazed into Harlyn's eyes. She studied him, trying to read his innermost thoughts. She'd spent many nights falling asleep to the picture-perfect image of the five of them running around the ranch, a happy family. She chuckled inwardly, reminding herself not to fall for the handsome cowboy.

"Just perfect," Kathy murmured while examining the smaller picture that included Harlyn.

"Aw, thank you. I like it when my photos bring others happiness."

"Oh, dear, I was talking about the people in the photo, but your photography skills are impeccable, too." Katy winked at Harlyn.

"The kids are adorable," Harlyn admired, ignoring Katy's other comment.

She'd already memorized all of Damon's features in the photograph. His deep brown eyes popped against the button-up, stretching across his chest. She could still feel her hip scorching where his hand rested the night she was at his cabin.

Life was cruel sometimes. Why couldn't God have given her someone like Damon? Ever since they'd spent more time together working or playing with his kids, he'd become softer and less grumpy. He still argued agricultural points with her, but slight twitches on his lips and a sparkle in his eyes led her to believe he wanted to get a rise out of her.

"Let's stop at the diner for dinner. My treat since you spent your entire day keeping me company."

Katy smiled. "It was my pleasure." She began texting. Harlyn assumed she was letting her husband, Jeff, know she wouldn't be home for dinner.

This woman warmed Harlyn's heart—like the mother she'd never had but wished for. She hadn't spent much time with Jeff, but he also seemed like a great man.

It'd taken twenty minutes to reach the diner. Dinner couldn't come quickly enough. She'd skipped lunch and drove like a mad woman to leave the ranch when she overheard Tanner and Damon talking in the barn.

Her stomach soured, recalling Damon's words. *"I'm not looking for a wife. I have kids to raise. I'm not going to waste my time."*

Had Harlyn read his kindness and more gentle demeanor wrong? Who was she kidding? Damon wasn't available regardless of how many smoldering looks he gave her. He had the perfect setup here—women to help raise his kids, buddies, and horses. There was no room for her in his life.

Damon wasn't willing to take another chance on love? Fine. She'd been alone this long. She could handle anything the good Lord put in her path. Besides, no matter what Quinton or Damon said, it was only a matter of time before she'd have to leave again. Brockton made it clear that he would never let her go.

Katy was like royalty at the dinner. Violet was the first to stop by the table and reintroduce herself to Harlyn. She didn't know what it was like to work, and given the stress oozing from the florist as she spoke with Katy, Harlyn didn't want to know.

Harlyn was shocked to learn that Violet had a thing for Sean, Raddix's dad. He's visited her flower shop weekly for over a year. Katy didn't seem surprised. Did she know if Sean reciprocated Violet's feelings? Though Harlyn had met Sean, he was reticent and to himself.

Violet skedaddled as the Troublesome Trio shuffled toward Harlyn and Katy.

Smart. Unless she wanted assistance connecting with Sean, she should stay clear of these deceptively sweet women.

"Hello, ladies, how are you?" Doris greeted them with a skip in her step.

"I'm fine, how about you?" Katy and Harlyn replied in unison.

"I'm not okay. Some, *I'm too good for this town preppy punk* thought he could bully me into giving him information."

Harlyn and Katy raised their eyebrows, urging her to continue.

"He wanted to know where you were, Dear."

"Me!?" Goosebumps formed on Harlyn's body, making her shiver.

A glance outside confirmed a black Mercedes Benz parked in the lot.

Harlyn's lungs seized. Brockton had found her. The man who'd wanted her as a trophy wife, who'd spent the better part of ten years following her around the country but never really bothering her. She saw his smug look in the big window as he passed, headed for the entrance.

Lord, please protect us. Maybe I should have kept the bodyguards? I just wanted to live a normal life.

Before she could say anything, Katy was already talking to Jeff. "Get to the diner. He found Harlyn."

Did everyone at the ranch know her story?

"Don't worry, Dear, help is on the way."

Katy's words did little to comfort her when Brockton entered the diner. This wasn't good. Harlyn's Grandpa told her never to marry Brockton, and she couldn't think of any other reason why he would be here. If she was being honest, Brockton should have moved on from her a long time ago, but he hadn't. That made Harlyn very leary. She had to find her Grandpa's secrets, figuring it would reveal Brockton's obsession with her. What did he know that she didn't?

The clanging of forks on plates made her jump. Looking around, she recognized many of the men as Amelia's ranchhands. Even the men she didn't know were standing, ready to stick up for her, making her heart swell.

"You don't know who I am," Brockton told the men. "If you touch me, you'll wish you were dead when I ruin you."

Yeah, Brockton was a big deal in the financial world back in Connecticut, but it's not like he could do anything to these men, right?

"Leave them alone," Harlyn barked at Brockton. "You are not welcome here; leave now."

Brockton moved toward Harlyn but stopped when seven cowboys formed a wall in the space between him and her.

Harlyn couldn't see anything except for the slimeball's shiny shoes.

The bell above the diner's door jingled, and a familiar voice filled the space. "Do we have a problem here?"

"No, sheriff." One of the cowboys crossed his arms over his chest. "This trespasser was just leaving."

"Trespasser? Are you for real? Isn't this a public establishment? I'm here for dinner," Brockton argued.

"Was that before or after you threatened us?" Myrtle exclaimed from her seat.

"That's nonsense. I just came here to bring my wife home. If you kindly move, I'll grab her and get out of his two-bit town before I catch something."

The collective gasps in the diner rang through Harlyn's ears.

Wife, ha! Harlyn would never be his wife even if her Grandpa hadn't told her not to marry him.

"You'd be lucky to catch some manners," Doris reared from behind the cowboy wall."

Rage and fear swept over her all at once. Harlyn's throat tightened. How could she fight against him and her parents? She'd rather submerge her hand in photo acid than deal with their repercussions.

Harlyn's chair squeaked against the tile floor as she stood. Parting the way between two of the tallest cowboys, she faced Brockton.

The cruel intent in Brockton's eyes made her shudder.

Her chest tightened. Panic zipped through her stomach as it dropped, rendering her nauseous.

Gathering her courage, she swallowed hard. "I am not your wife and never will be. You need to leave."

The door flung open, and her body throbbed. Every one of Damon's muscles popped, and his jaw tensed. His eyes filled with fury as he stared down Brockton.

A little flutter in her stomach caught her attention. Damon, in protective mode, was hot. She met his gaze and held it. His eyes softened, almost as if he were asking if she was okay. This made her ache for him, for his security—a new feeling that scared her a little, if she was being honest.

Her smile must have reassured him.

He charged forward, directing his attention back on Brockton, but Jeff, Quinton, Raddix, and the sheriff stopped him.

"He looks angrier than the Broncs he used to ride. You better what out, Dude," one of the cowboys creating the wall declared.

"Hold up, Cowboy. No need to fight. That," pointing to Harlyn, "is my wife. I'll take her out of your hair and go."

Doris pushed her way through the cowboys behind Harlyn. "First of all, young fella, Harlyn is a human; don't refer to her as *that*. Second, you are never taking her as your wife."

"Yeah, old lady, what makes you so sure?"

Doris shook herself into a frenzy. She dragged the closest chair along, stopping in front of Brockton. She used his shoulder to hoist herself onto the chair seat to be at eye level with him. Surprisingly, he hadn't flinched at her touch.

Two of the cowboys flanked Doris on either side.

She poked one of her long fingers into his chest. "You young man are a disgrace. No. You're a pompous jerk and don't deserve our sweet Harlyn."

Brockton brushed her finger away with a flick of his fingers. "That's my wife, and there's nothing you, or any of these hillbillies, can do about it."

He stepped around the chair, only to be blocked by the other cowboys who came forward between Harlyn and Doris.

"Harlyn, you're just making this worse on yourself."

She was used to the misery and didn't care about herself. But the people of Haven Ridge are innocent. Being woven into this toxic situation was the last thing Harlyn wanted for any of them.

"That sounds like a threat, Sheriff."

"Shut up, you old hag."

Myrtle swung her purse, smacking the schmuck's arm.

Harlyn loved Doris so much. She could pull any antics she wanted as long as she kept hitting him.

Brockton turned toward the sheriff. "I want to press assault charges against this woman."

Gerard cleared his throat. "Excuse me, folks. Did anyone see this elderly lady attack this strapping young man?"

A chorus of *nos* filled the diner. The loyalty. Harlyn's heart was a soupy mess.

"Get going before her real husband takes care of you," Myrtle silenced the room.

What was she doing? Harlyn hoped the flurry of emotions racing through her body wasn't evident on her face.

"Excuse me? She is my wife."

Myrtle shot him a sly smile. "She can't be your wife when she's already married." The woman winked at Damon.

"Is that so? She's been promised to me." Turning toward Harlyn, his eyes bore into her. "Your parents won't be happy to hear this.

Myrtle, what are you getting me into? Lord, Please just let him go away. Harlyn couldn't breathe. This wasn't going to end well. Her stomach dipped again. Avoiding her destiny was pointless. Trying to be happy was pointless.

Maybe she should have given in to that life so none of these good people get hurt.

Then her heart skittered when Damon stepped forward, declaring, "As of today, she's my wife, and if you don't leave now, no one in this diner will be able to save you."

Swoon alert. The inside of Harlyn's stomach tickled. This was the same man who argued with her about wrapping trees. How did we become husband and wife?

Brockton stared around at all the people protecting Harlyn. She couldn't believe that an entire town had stuck up for her, and Damon, was he nuts?

His voice dripped with malice as he pointed at Harlyn. "This is not over. Wait until your parents hear this." He shifted toward Damon. "We'll destroy you, Cowboy. Enjoy your last night with her; she'll be in my bed soon."

Brockton shoved the door open, stomping like a spoiled child. He squealed his tires as he left the diner. *Thank you, God!*

Harlyn pinned her atomic fireball eyes on Damon. *What was he thinking?* She rushed toward him. The entire diner cheered and hollered, offering congratulations. Damon enveloped her hand, sending starbursts through her fingers. Harlyn caught Hazel and Myrtle smiling and winking at her from the corner. Myrtle mouthed, "Go with it. You're welcome."

"He's more charming than I thought," Damon joked, only for her to hear. "Does he have a sister? I'm sure Tanner would love some drama like that."

Chapter 13

Harlyn: Nineteen-Years-Old

With red-rimmed eyes, Harlyn squeezed her grandpa's hand. Fading fast, he requested *time alone with his granddaughter.* According to what Grandpa told her, Nancy hadn't liked it, but she didn't have much of a choice.

"Grandpa. You can't die. You have to get better. How am I going to survive without you?"

"You will leave tomorrow in my motorhome." He took a deep breath. "I'm ready to go home and be with your grandmother." She'd passed away a half of a decade earlier.

"Don't contest anything in my will. I left everything in my name to your mother."

"What?! Why?"

"There isn't much left in my name, maybe a million dollars. She'll need it when all is said and done. She's not stupid, though. There's so much more. She will never stop looking for it, hence you."

Her heart shattered like it had a year ago when her plan to leave had crumbled.

Nancy's attorney had contacted Grandpa's, revealing some stipulations in the family inheritance paperwork. She remembered reading the text aloud like it was yesterday.

> Harold, we have an issue. New verbiage has appeared in the family inheritance.
>
> "If any heir leaves the home or marries before his/her nineteenth birthday, he/she forfeits any claim to the Summer's inheritance."

Harlyn hadn't cared then and still didn't care now about her inheritance. She only stayed because her grandpa asked her to, reminding her never to marry Brockton and avoid marriage until the Lord convicted her. It was then that Harlyn realized her mother never took her father's surname because she was greedy—her name was worth more.

If Harlyn were a crier, this would have been a safe place—with her Grandpa, but he didn't need to see her sadness. She'd have plenty of time when he was gone, like the rest of her life, to mourn him.

"Your grandmother blamed herself for the way your mother turned out. It wasn't that dear, sweet woman's fault, and it's not your fault either. Never forget that."

Harlyn couldn't forget it because her grandparents told her this every time she saw them.

"Your mother fell in love with money early on and wanted more. Our family's money corrupted her quickly. What she plans to do with it is a secret to everyone. That heel of a man she married wasn't any better."

"What do I need to know for my departure?" Harlyn's determination was evident.

"One. Listen to the spirit. When it says *move*, make sure you do. When it says, *be still*, freeze."

That's all she'd heard for the last year. The stillness nearly paralyzed her.

"Two. Never marry Brockton. EVER! It will change the family dynamics, and it won't be pretty. Trust me. Choose wisely if you do marry someone. If you don't, it will go badly for you and your children." She did trust him, and she didn't want to marry the slimeball, so no problem there. She'd probably never marry after seeing her parent's life.

"Was my mother ever humane?"

Grandpa chuckled. "Yes." His eyes softened as if remembering fondly.

"She married young. Your dad learned how much power he had, and Nancy refused to let him have it." Tears pooled in his eyes. "I lost my baby girl because she didn't listen. Please don't repeat history."

"I won't, Grandpa," Harlyn rested her head on his chest, hoping muscle memory would always help her feel his warm embrace. "Is there anything else?"

"Yes, but you'll have to figure it out on your own, I can't share it with you."

"How?"

"Here are the keys to the motorhome." He reached into his nightstand drawer and pulled out an envelope. Grandpa had returned a week ago, wanting to spend his last days on Earth in his bed.

"Thank you, Grandpa. I still don't understand how this is part of the plan."

"This is the title to the motorhome—it's yours. You must leave tonight."

The determination in his eyes put her on high alert.

"Do not tarry, or that will be another nail in your coffin, giving your mother more control than she should have."

"Grandpa, you're being very cryptic. Please just spell it out for me," Harlyn begged.

"I overheard your mother talking on the phone." She gave him an incredulous look. "I'm a good fake sleeper." He shrugged. "Brockton is planning the proposal—don't give him the opportunity."

"Okay." Harlyn trusted her Grandpa with everything. Maybe because of that, she knew there was more to his directions.

"Never give this motorhome away or sell it until you find your freedom." She tried to ask a question, but Grandpa pushed on through. "Even if . . . err, rather when they coming searching for you, just keep moving to another place. They will pressure you to marry Brockton, but staying away is the key to your freedom."

"What am I looking for?"

He coughed when the excited hitch in his voice was too much. Then he pulled out a necklace with a key dangling from the end. Tears stung the back of Harlyn's eyes.

"My necklace. I thought I'd never see this again. Grandma said this would save my life." God had put Winnie in a position to save Harlyn that birthday so many years ago.

"Winnie returned it to your grandmother before she left, and we decided it was safer to hold onto it for you. That key fits something in the motorhome. Once you find it, ultimate freedom is yours, one way or another. God will lead you to it when the time is right. Trust God and never leave Him. He'll never leave you."

The seriousness of his eyes sent chills down Harlyn's back. Her mother was ruthless. Harlyn had the scars, physical and emotional, to prove it.

"I'm going to be alone forever, aren't I?"

"No, honey. I feel it in my bones. There's a man out there for you. God is just preparing him for you." His eyes softened for a brief moment.

She leaned over, resting her head on his chest, and she let out a soft sob.

"You'll be fine, my strong beauty. Open the envelope." He pointed toward his stand.

She gingerly ran her finger underneath the flap.

"This is the name of my financial guy." Harlyn looked at the name Stan Windshire. "I acquired him when your mother started claiming my money." Harlyn remembered. He hadn't even gotten sick yet. "He's top-notch and honest."

Harlyn pulled out the paper—a certificate showing seventy million dollars—and Grandpa's account had been transferred to her. Her eyes bugged out of her head.

"This is a new bank account your mother doesn't know exists." The triumphant smile on his face warmed Harlyn's heart. Stan made me twenty million dollars in the last eighteen months. I'd only given him fifty to work with."

"Only?' she blew out a hard breath.

"Well, you know what I mean. I only tell you this to show you he's good at his job. He and Richard expect you at that address in just a few hours. They have bodyguards ready for you." Her Grandpa coughed violently.

Once his lungs settled back down, he continued. "You can live off the interest alone every month. If you choose not to work, you can, but I hope you continue with your photography."

Harlyn's Grandpa died that night.

Returning to her room, Harlyn packed a suitcase and her camera equipment. Winnie had filled the motorhome with food, so Harlyn wouldn't have to stop for hours.

"Come with me," Harlyn begged, knowing she'd never see this beloved woman again.

"No, Dear. That'll make it worse for you and everyone else here in the long run. Your mother will think everyone helped you escape, and they will pay for it. I couldn't live with that."

They hugged. "I'm sorry I have to leave you."

"Never be sorry. We want you to get far, far away, and never come back. We love you and know you are destined for great things. Take some great pictures, JCLH."

"Huh?"

"Jesus Christ loves Harlyn." Tears escape from both ladies' eyes.

Harlyn's pseudonym for her photo entries was born that day.

"Now, go before they catch you. You were born into a dumpster fire, but Jesus is now walking you out of it; follow Him to greatness."

Chapter 14

"Are you crazy?!" Harlyn growled in his ear, making him cringe. "When exactly did we get married?"

"Well, keep yelling at me, wifey, and people will think we got hitched years ago." He tried to joke to ease the tension, but it felt all wrong. Could he pretend to be married to this beauty who's ransacked his thoughts? He wasn't supposed to be attracted to anyone. His only job was to raise his children. Her backhanded *lovetap* to the gut didn't feel great either.

Damon recoiled, unsure what to say. Anger had flooded his body, and he couldn't stand listening to that uppity dirtbag one more minute. Besides, he wanted to protect Harlyn. His kids were attached to her, and he didn't want them to lose another woman.

"Help me down fellas," Doris requested. She squeezed the tallest cowboy's muscles once her feet were firmly on the ground. "Thank you, Handsome."

The men returned to their dinners, chuckling at the older woman's antics.

"We can't get married, Damon." Harlyn dropped her face into her hand. "I. . . we barely know each other, and . . ."

He lifted his hands. "And what?"

Sadness filled her eyes, piercing his insides. "You said it yourself. You're not looking for a wife. You've got kids to raise, and I'm a waste of your time." She crossed her arms over her chest.

"Did you say that, Man?" Sheriff McDugal shook his head and sucked in a long, low breath before walking away.

Damon searched her face. He'd only known her a few weeks, but he'd never seen her look vulnerable. Her strong, often stubborn personality was what got them arguing. Her expression now made him feel like a heel. He'd fix it somehow and make her feel strong again. Damon reached out for her with his other hand but pulled back quickly and stuffed his hands in his pockets.

He hadn't meant for anyone, especially Harlyn, to hear his conversation with Tanner. That statement was more about his own insecurity than anything.

"I didn't mean what I said. Well, I meant it, but not maliciously like you're taking it."

"Is there any other way to take it when someone says you're not worth their time?"

That wasn't exactly what I had said, but he learned long ago not to have a war of words with a woman, she'd win every time.

Instead, he'd show her that wasn't what he meant. Damon cupped her elbow and guided Harlyn outside. The frigid night air whooshed over her, causing her to shiver visibly. He took off his button-up and wrapped it on her shoulders. "Sorry, it's not heavier. We left the ranch right when Katy called."

'Thank you." She pulled the sides tighter over her chest.

Damon paced the parking lot in front of Harlyn. He rested his hand low on his hips and ran his other hand through his hair.

"My wife left. I couldn't make or keep her happy—"

She stopped him with her raised palm. He paused, trying to read her thoughts. No use in that—another thing he'd learned long ago.

Harlyn scoffed, "So I'll ask again, are you crazy? Why would you say you're married to me if, by your own admission, you're not a good husband?"

Ouch. There it was. Her directness. She never had a problem calling him out.

"I don't know." Damon shrugged. "Call it divine intervention. Think of it as God speaking through me." He kicked the dirt with his foot. "It's not like it's real, but at least you'll be safe from that maniac." Damon pointed in the direction Brockton sped away.

"So romantic. I wonder if our honeymoon will be as thrilling?" Harlyn huffed.

A sly smile grew slowly over Damon's features. "There's going to be a honeymoon?"

"If we do this, there will be no marital privileges, kissing, or touching at all," Harlyn clarified.

"That's a surefire way for everyone to believe the marriage is legit." Cheryl had pulled away from intimacy, so it was not a foreign feeling to Damon, just a miserable one.

"Oh, *now* you have a sense of humor!" Harlyn gripped her hips, and much to Damon's surprise, his mind drifted to the night Harlyn read Darlene a bedtime story, and Harlyn splashed her palms on his chest. His hand landed on the same spot on her hips that night. Blissful.

He shook his head, hoping the smoke billowing low in his belly wouldn't ignite into a full-fledged inferno.

"Truthfully, there must be some touching for this to be believable," Damon reasoned.

"I don't even know if I'm allowed to get married."

Damon's brows shot up. "Allowed?"

She explained her Grandpa's directions and warnings ten years ago before she left that awful mansion.

"Wow, I don't know what to think. From what you say, you can get married as long as it's not Brockton and you're over nineteen, but whatever family secret you don't even know—will be tied to your husband."

"Exactly."

His heart started to race. He didn't want more drama, but he couldn't imagine Harlyn dealing with this alone. Her controlling parents, the dirtbag they betrothed her to—it all sounded like a cult. Harlyn's reserved expression reminded him of a five-alarm dumpster fire. She was keeping something from him. How worse could it get? What if marrying to protect her now hurt her later, or him? The kids? He'd never do anything to harm his kids.

"What about the diner full of people who just witnessed this out of the blue? I think they'll know we're lying about getting married."

"Did you hear all the cowboys cheering for us? They think we're already married. We only have to worry about the sheriff, the men from the ranch, Myrtle, Doris, Hazel, and Frank by association—he knows so much more than he lets on."

"What are you doing to tell your kids?"

That did it. Kids were the best fire extinguisher this side of Heaven. They could get an annulment or divorce before anything her Grandpa hadn't shared affected the kids, right? Would he be okay if they had to stay married forever so that Harlyn could stay safe? Based on what he knew now, his answer was a resounding yes. Did that mean the kids didn't have to know the truth? Darlene already loves her, and the boys have only had good things to report from when she helped out at school.

They've already lost their mother. Maybe this wouldn't be a good plan after all. Ideas were bouncing

"What are you getting out of this?"

"This isn't about me, Harlyn."

"If you could put on your big boy briefs and tell me, this would be much easier."

He huffed out a breath. Maybe she was right. *Walk away* played on repeat in his head, but if feet were cinder blocks, he had two. "See, I know that I'm no one's *happily ever after,* and I've grown to live with that, but I can be a temporary prince charming to keep you from that dirtbag. Besides, we won't even have to get married." He was so sure of himself until he saw her vexed eyes.

Pity? Sadness? Intimation? He's sure he saw a combination of all three rolled into her eyes, now a blueish-green combo, reminding him of the water in one of Harlyn's photographs of a tropical island.

"My kids like you, so we tell them we got married—it will be real to them." Damon sighed when she didn't respond. "You can't leave with Brockton, whatever his name is. What choice do you have?"

"You don't know them. I'm sure Brockton is searching for marriage licenses given out in Haven Ridge as we speak. He'll be back once he realizes you lied." She wrapped her arms around her middle. "Then what about your kiddos? They'll be devastated when another woman walks out on them. I can't do that to them, Damon. I won't. Even if I didn't already think they were amazing, no child deserves that treatment."

If he hadn't already respected Harlyn, that just did it. She cared about his kid's well-being. He should have taken that wimp out with one punch. Since he didn't, now he would make it his life's mission to keep Harlyn safe and replace the distressed look on her face with the brightness he'd been used to seeing. There would be worse things than staying married to Harlyn for the rest of his life. If she could put up with him, he'd do whatever it took to keep Brockton out of her life.

"To answer your earlier question, this arrangement will work well for me if you accept the mission." He laughed, trying to build up his nerve.

"The women on the ranch are great, but they are not the kid's mother," he paused long enough for Harlyn to respond.

"Neither am I." Harlyn pressed the heels of her hands into her eyes. "I've never been a mom nor had any good parental role models."

"Well, just do the opposite then," he said, feigning a smile. "Seriously, I need a mother for my kiddos who'll be there for them whenever they are in need. I try, but I'm not motherly." She already cared more about the kid's well-being than their biological mother—she'd be great.

"You don't say, Oscar." His confused look had her shaking her head. "The Grouch from Sesame Street."

"Funny."

"So you don't want anything else?"

Damon thought back to his childhood. His mom always cared for him and his dad's needs—she made their lunches and dinners, cleaned their clothes, and kissed Dad before he left.

As if she could read my mind, she said, "I mean, you could think of me as the maid and nanny." Her eyes widened like she just had an epiphany. "I'll have to move into your cabin, won't I?"

He blew out an expected breath of laughter. "That's usually how it works."

His nerves ratcheted up. Sleeping arrangements would need to be believable. He could sleep on the floor or, if lucky, on top of the covers.

The sheriff stuck his head out the door. "Could you two meet me in the kitchen, please?"

Damon gestured for Harlyn to go first, placing his hand low on her back, just enough for her to squirm away.

"No touching, remember?"

"I am, first and foremost, a gentleman, and we are in public, so you'll have to get used to this, honey bun."

Where had that come from? There was a time when he had been fun and flirty. Maybe this situation could bring back those parts of him—a benefit to the kids, as well.

When they arrived at the door, he reached over her shoulder, pressing his chest to her back. He put his hand over hers, preventing her from opening it. He leaned in close, her apple shampoo filling his senses.

His lips grazed her skin as he spoke. "Just so you know, I wear boxers, not briefs, which you're about to find out because that's what I sleep in. Welcome to marriage, Sweetheart."

Chapter 15

Two years hadn't been enough time away. Brockton kept finding her. Eight months ago, he cornered her in a rest-stop bathroom. That was when Stan and Richard, her Grandpa's—err, her financial advisor and attorney made her hire two more bodyguards.

As they pulled off the highway, the bodyguards turned into Rambo. Two scouted the area first. When they returned, they stayed at the motorhome while four others escorted Harlyn to the bathroom. Two stayed outside the bathroom door with Harlyn, while the other two searched the bathroom first, disregarding any shrieks from within.

"Where are we?" Harlyn asked Ryder, the closest guard.

"Just outside Indiana."

"All clear," Mike reported as he opened the door.

Harlyn entered with Mike and another guard following her. They waited by the door until Harlyn was finished.

Was all this really necessary? She wasn't the president or a famous singer or actor getting threatening notes. This many bodyguards was over the top, or so she thought. Her grandpa had said that whatever she didn't know was to protect her. *Argh!*

She hadn't complained when she first met her guards. They were all the strong, handsome type. Five of the six were married, which made Harlyn feel bad for their wives and families. How long would she need body-guards?

It baffled her that Brockton would chase her down two years later. Her Grandpa's words returned to her, *"There isn't much left in my name, maybe a million dollars. She'll need it when all is said and done. She's not stupid, though. There's so much more. She will never stop looking for it, hence you."*

So, that answered some of her questions, but she still had so many unanswered ones. How was Brockton finding her? Scott, the head bodyguard, hadn't found any trackers on or in the motorhome. Could he have someone following them, and that's how he could show up randomly? Anything was possible, but she hated the thought.

A more profound frustration for her was the key that she rubbed between her fingers. *What does this open?* Her Grandpa told her that whatever it opened would give her ultimate freedom. Richard also seemed to know what it opened, but he promised Harold he wouldn't tell until a designated time. He wouldn't share that time either. *Good grief.*

Harlyn relaxed on the leather bench seat connected to a small square table in the motorhome. Mike sat across from her while Rob, Finn, and Ryder relaxed on the couch. Scott drove, and Matt rode shotgun this leg of the trip. They were all former military personnel—three SEALs, one Green Beret, and two Marines. The heckling amongst them was funny for the first year; now, it's annoying, but she doesn't say much since they are protecting her.

"It's hard to imagine someone with your background can remain so faithful," Mike pointed to her open Bible on the table.

"I couldn't imagine not believing. Things would be so much worse if I eliminated God from my life," Harlyn declared.

She studied him for a moment. "Don't you believe? I imagine He's saved you many times."

"Of course, Mike's a SEAL," Rob taunted. "He couldn't do anything on his own."

Mike whipped around, "And you could, Mr. Marine? How many Special ops were you involved in?"

Silence.

"That's what I thought. Why don't you call your wife, or can't she stand you, either?"

Harlyn never knew when they were teasing. Mike sounded serious, but Rob just laughed.

Returning his attention to Harlyn, Mike asked, "What are your future plans?"

She stared out the window into the dark of night—seemingly appropriate. She felt like she was clawing her way through the dark every day she went to sleep without answers. "I guess I plan to stay away from my parents and the Jenkles."

"Obviously. Will you ever get married, have a family, or have a photography career? It's not that you need to work."

She chortled, "You're funny."

"Looks aren't everything," Finn interjected, and Mike threw a stress ball at the guard's head.

"That's all great for someone not hiding away from crazy people. Besides, you're the only single man I've interacted with in the last two years, so finding someone to marry is doubtful."

"Burn." The guys on the couch fist-bumped one another, making it difficult for Harlyn to know who spoke.

Harlyn felt bad. Was Mike trying to let her know that he was interested in her? She couldn't date him. He's here trying to protect her. He was handsome enough. Without complaint, she could wake up to him for the rest of her life, but that didn't seem right to the other guards, who wanted more time with their families. This quick trip through Indiana allowed Scott and Ryder to see their families briefly before continuing west.

"I want to marry, but finding a woman who can handle this lifestyle is difficult."

Harlyn's eyes softened. "Mmm-hmm. I can imagine." She smiled. "You know, the Bible says that married people will have many troubles, so maybe you're better off remaining single. At least for me. I don't need any more trouble."

Chapter 16

"Relax, would you?" Damon entered his bathroom.

Sure. That was easy for him to do. Kissing her cheek, almost, and talking about underwear must be an everyday occurrence for him. It wasn't a kiss—that would have stopped her heart. Dead—but instead, it was a sweet brush against her skin.

I can't imagine what a real kiss with him would be like. If he'd kept contact any longer, he would have had to start CPR. Nope, she'd never come back from a kiss.

Stop it! She chastised herself. *Don't focus on his lips, underwear, or anything below his hairline and you'll survive.*

Now she stood at the foot of his bed, checking her watch, wondering how she'd become Mrs. Damon Richards a mere fifty-seven minutes ago.

It all came rushing back to her like the Great Flood in the Nineties. Her self-proclaimed photography mentor, Lisa Liberty, had won a Pulitzer for her picture of the Air Force Base drowning in that catastrophe.

Drowning? She knew something about that, thanks to her mother. Right now, her lungs burned. Her vocal cords spasmed, sealing her airway and making it impossible for her to speak. Yes, she was drowning in a sea of emotion—she was married, and it wasn't to Brockton, *thank God*, but a handsome cowboy with manners.

Had she messed up everything Grandpa had planned?

The last hour replayed through her mind. The three wonderful grandmas, A.K.A. The Troublesome Trio certainly earned their name. Before she and Damon entered the kitchen, they had a marriage license ready to sign.

Coincidentally, Hazel was a notary and Myrtle an officiant, which was *very convenient*. Katy and Jeff were the witnesses.

"Whatever we do," Quinton spoke about the congratulations, "don't let any of the kids know this isn't real, especially Emmanuel."

Damon explained that gray did not exist in Emmanuel's world. His little neurodivergent buddy had many strengths, especially empathy. He had more in his pinky finger than most adults had in their entire bodies. The concern was that he told things how they were in the clearest manner possible so the secret would be out instantly.

Harlyn wished gray didn't exist in her world as she finally climbed into bed, hoping there wasn't a particular side he wanted. She pulled the covers up to her chest.

The bathroom door slowly creaked open. She didn't dare look. The idea of him sleeping in just his boxers next to her was . . .

Before she could finish her thought, he sang out. "Mrs. Richards, I'm ready for bed."

He was having way too much fun at her expense. *Where had the grump gone?*

Sadly, she owed him. He didn't have a clue what he was up against. Her parents and Brockton would be back with a vengeance.

Against her better judgment, she asked, "I thought you slept in your boxers?"

Not that the tight t-shirt and pajama shorts were any less attractive, snug to his respective muscles.

"You complaining? Mrs. Richards, you devil."

Her breath hitched as a kaleidoscope of butterflies fluttered around her stomach. She was in way over her head. In seconds, she went from a single lady to a married mom.

Damon headed across the room to a wooden chest built into the wall underneath one of the windows. When he lifted the lid, the hinges cried under the pressure. The most beautiful quilt she'd ever seen had been hidden away in there.

"Wow, that's gorgeous."

"I am even more stunning in my boxers." He winked. "I thought you might need some time to work up to seeing that. Was I wrong?" This teasing tone pulled Harlyn in.

Harlyn enjoyed this side of Damon. Granted, he'd been a little grumpy with her at times, but even when they were battling each other, the air around them had an electrifying sizzle that she never noticed when he argued with others.

"Yes." She shook her head. "I mean, no." He flustered her like no one ever had. She steeled her emotions. "I'm sure you are irresistible in your boxers, but I was referring to the quilt." Harlyn composed herself.

"Oh, right. Thanks. My mom made it before I got married the first time." He shouldered it to his side of the bed. "Pull your quilt a little more your way."

"Why?"

"When I lie on top of it, you won't move me, and I don't want you to be cold," he stated casually. He turned off the light once she moved the quilt her way.

Aw. She knew he could be sweet, but it wasn't nice of him to start being nice to her now that she had to lay so close to him. The mattress dipped where he sat. As he moved around, her body jostled back and forth. He finally settled, mere centimeters away from her. *Breathe.* She let out a slow, quiet breath.

"You alright?" She heard the playfulness in his voice.

"Mmm-hmm," was all she dared to say.

Earlier, when he'd hugged her during their marriage ceremony, he whispered, "I know you said no touching, but we have to unite somehow, and I figured you'd mind this the least."

Mind? No, she hadn't minded his warm breath on her cheek again or being in his arms. She'd felt like she belonged there. God had made that spot at the top of his chest perfect for her head to rest comfortably, and her arms wrapped nicely around his strong, lean core. He'd pulled away too quickly, leaving her longing for the protection of his embrace.

She lay on her side, her hands pressed against one another, secured safely underneath her chin, staring at her husband.

She prayed silently for their safety as she watched him stare at the ceiling.

"We didn't discuss this, but are we going to divorce when Brockton and your parents give up."

Oh, poor Damon. She felt terrible for him. He thought he'd have an out. It would be nice if it were only a waiting game, but she knew it wasn't. As long as they were alive, her past would always haunt them.

"Sure." She hated giving him false hope, knowing he didn't want a wife, but being blunt this time didn't feel right either.

He rested his hands behind his head. Did guys know their muscles popped, thus making them look all the more irresistible when they did that? Of course, they did. She wouldn't let that keep her from learning what she wanted to know.

"In all sincerity, what do I need to do to make sure I'm not a waste of your time?"

He slowly turned his head toward her first, then shifted his entire body to his side. His eyes pinned her down with something akin to interest flowing through them.

She lifted her eyes, challenging him to answer honestly.

"That statement was stupid. Just guy talk. At the time, I was thinking about how Cheryl had left me. I'd wasted my time trying to make her happy when, in the end, she left anyway."

A strand of hair slipped over her eye. He reached out and tucked behind her ear, heating her skin with his fingertips in their wake.

"So, hopefully, you see, it was more of a pity party or a slam against my abilities and not an insult toward you. I am honored to call you my wife."

Tears pooled in her eyes. She'd never been so thankful for the nearly darkened room with only a streak of moonlight shining through the break in the curtain.

She could only imagine his pain. Cheryl was the love of his life, and she'd left. Harlyn had prayed endless hours that Brockton and her parents would leave her, but they were like the annoying gnats that always found her. Squashing one of them wouldn't be enough because the others would take its place until they were all eliminated. The thought made Harlyn shutter. She couldn't *eliminate* people. She prayed every night and multiple times daily that God would wipe those three gnats off the planet as fast as he produced the creatures during the Ten Plagues.

Her breath picked up. Harlyn's palms covered her face, needing a moment without the cowboy's intense eyes boring into her. She might not see all that well in the dark, but she could feel him.

She was married to a man who was emotionally unavailable and physically appealing. It was a horrible combination—terrible. Why did God choose *now* to show he had a sense of humor?

Damon wrapped his rough, sturdy hands around her wrist, pulling her arm to her side.

"Are you okay?"

That was a vexed question. Sure, she was okay if that meant marrying a handsome cowboy with sweet tendencies.

On the other hand, she was *not* okay, knowing she endangered all these lovely people at the ranch.

"We'll never be able to divorce. They're never going away," Harlyn whispered, sharing the reality of their situation.

"Neither will I."

What!? It's not fair for him to say things like that. Desire flared in her core. Her heart soared.

She swallowed repeatedly, hoping her emotion wasn't evident when she asked, "What will you tell your kids in the morning?"

Damon smirked, "I just had to marry you, so I did. My boys will understand the biblical meaning." His low, gravelly voice increased her desire growing within. "Darlene will probably just be happy to have another woman around."

"Don't count on that. She enjoys being the only girl," Harlyn said, not wanting to reveal the entirety of the girl's secret.

Damon chuckled, "For room purposes, maybe, but you'll be sharing my room, so she's out of luck."

A surge of excitement needled through her body, warming her all over.

Don't read into his words. Thinking of him as anything more than a legally bound bodyguard in a cowboy hat and stunning boxers (which she will most definitely never see) was as deadly as her trying to become a Bronc rider.

"Tell me. Are those scars I saw on your ribs earlier from your riding days?"

"Checking me out without my shirt, I see?" She heard the smile in his voice.

"Not really. You pulled your shirt off before you shut the bathroom door. It's pretty big, so it was hard to miss."

"If that's your story." He had the nerve to chuckle at her.

"Want to see it up close?"

No. Maybe. "Sure," she kept her voice as even as possible.

Harlyn grabbed her phone and pressed the flashlight icon, and her breath shuddered when Damon sat up, stretched his arms over his head, pulling his shirt over his head.

The vulnerable expression on his face tugged at her heart. Was he just as nervous and out of sorts as her?

The puckered skin ran underneath his pectoral muscle diagonal along his ribs, ending on his back.

"That looks painful."

"Death would have been worse."

"I suppose." Harlyn reached her hand out but stopped short of touching him.

Why did scars make men even more appealing? She continued to examine it with her eyes. This could get intimate real quick. Haryln was drawn to him like a bull to a red flag.

"You can touch it. It doesn't hurt anymore."

She studied the scar and of course the surrounding area, how could she not? Thinking better, only by the grace of God, she replied, "I'm good. Thanks, though."

As if he'd been reading her thoughts, he stated, "I've heard that women find scars sexy."

Harlyn giggled. "Who've you been talking to?"

He ignored her question. "You are my wife. You can't be squirmish around me." The amusement in his tone and his mischievous grin weren't lost on her.

She turned off the flashlight and returned her phone to the side table. Harlyn rolled onto her stomach. "Then I'd be breaking my own rule. I can't have that."

"No, of course not," sarcasm poured from his lips.

"How about you tell me what happened."

Harlyn listened intently as he shared the story of falling off the horse. It stepped on his ribs, breaking four of them. One of the broken ribs punctured his lung, which was only taken care of with emergency surgery.

"And you got back on a horse after that?'

She felt his throaty laugh reverberate through her body.

"I didn't think twice."

"Hmm."

Perhaps Cheryl hadn't appreciated Damon putting himself in danger. Maybe she couldn't handle the constant worrying. Perhaps he hadn't been as devoted to his family as he was now, and she hadn't liked that. If Damon had been the same man back then as he is now, Harlyn couldn't fathom Cheryl's reasoning for leaving, but something warranted her feelings.

"Do I want to know what you're thinking?"

"I don't think so, but I don't believe in secrets, especially between husband and wife."

After sharing her thoughts, Damon admitted that he'd learned much over the last decade.

"So, I'll benefit from all your wisdom," her tone, joking.

"That's the plan. I need to get some sleep. Goodnight, wife."

"Goodnight, husband."

She rolled the other way with a smile on her face. *Thank you, Lord.*

Chapter 17

Thank you, Lord, for keeping me safe. But I'll be honest, this is miserable. I was supposed to have my freedom. All I've done is run from one beautiful place to another. I want more out of life besides running.

Harlyn dreamed of having a handsome, loving husband who doted on her just as much as she did him. Their children were loved, and they knew it! She fingered the chain around her neck, holding the key her grandparents gave her. Even without this necklace, the money, and the motorhome, she knew they loved her by the way they spoke to her with a loving, caring tone. They stood up for her against her parents.

In the time Harlyn had been gone, her parents hadn't attempted to contact her at all. Why hadn't they loved her like parents should love their child? Heck, if she knew. Neither one of them spoke much about family. Her mother rarely acknowledged Grandma and Grandpa as her kin, let alone loving parents.

Only Brockton, the weasel, continued to hunt her down like a rabbit. At one time, she imagined someone might find Brockton handsome with his roughed-up, little longer hair that sometimes dipped over his eye. He was lean but had muscles that seemed impressive. But, all she saw was a slicked-haired, pompous, arrogant narcissist with ghastly features.

Harlyn shut her thinking down and sang along with the radio. It was one of the songs from Footloose. *How fitting, Lord. Thank you. I know you're still with me.* She couldn't help but smile.

"Shaking the past making my breaks

taking control, that's what it takes (I'm free!)

Heaven helps the man who fights his fear . . .

She was done with running. She missed out on pictures she wanted to take or things she wanted to do as she traveled the last few years because Brockton had shown his slimy face everywhere she went. How had he known where to find her?

Harlyn's dismal voice turned cheery, "Welcome to Arizona, the Grand Canyon State."

Lord, please give me the strength to stay the course. There is so much I want to do here. Please help the Spirit guide me.

As Harlyn pressed the power window button. The warm breeze blew through the space, releasing her of the pain and anger she'd held onto her entire life. She was tired of worrying about her parents and Brockton finding her. *I am so done with that!* Her mind screamed. So what if they did? She was an adult. They couldn't *make* her do anything she didn't want to do.

Richard urged her to get a new phone every two weeks. She'd done that for the past couple of years, but she grew tired of the hassle and stopped purchasing phones about a month ago, forcing all communication between them to go through email or her bodyguards.

Stan, her financial guy, as Grandpa called him, emailed her monthly statements. He was making her a killing, which she donated most to the photography scholarship program she'd set up. Recently, she started donating to an organization working with orphans and another helping women get out of dangerous situations.

Despite a few run-ins with Brockton at a theme park and an aquarium in Tennessee over a year ago, her bodyguards began trailing her in separate vehicles, letting her live her life without them hovering twenty-four-seven. Even though she hadn't seen hide or hair of Brockton since, everyone felt the protection was still necessary.

"Don't underestimate them," her Grandpa's words rang through her head.

She might be brave, but not stupid. She'd just given everyone at the security company a raise. Though they rotated the men every three months, meaning they only had two details a year, she imagined how difficult it'd been for them to leave their families for that time.

It didn't take long for Harlyn to determine that Central Arizona was by far her favorite place. It was a hot spot for retirees during the winter. Throughout the summer, the population ebbed considerably. For Harlyn, dry heat trumped humid heat any day, even when the temperature reached one hundred ten.

Today, she was trying to find anything in her motorhome that would fit her key. She exited her motorhome, and the bright sun scorched her skin. If she were a flower, she would have wilted by now. Since she'd been here so long, she had the best spot in the campsite—close to the manmade pond and easy access in and out.

Loneliness and frustration were getting the best of her. She'd never considered being like her winter campground neighbors Bob and Linda. Snowbirds, they called themselves, living in Arizona from the beginning of October to the end of April while living in Maine the rest of the time. They'd invited her to their camp in Kingfield.

Nothing—not even a sure Pulitzer win—could make Harlyn return to the Northeast.

She still hadn't won a Pulitzer, but it wasn't for lack of trying. Over the last nine months, she'd found ideal spots in Arizona and entered ten photos in different contests.

Yesterday, Richard called to let her know that one of the photographs he entered for her had earned her another Prix Pictet, furthering her scholarship foundation.

Frustration bubbled inside her because she still hadn't found what her key opened. She thought leaving the mansion would have set her free, but she was a prisoner now just as much as when she was under her parent's thumb, sort of.

Yeah, she was in an elaborate motorhome, traveling the country, but she was always watching her back, waiting for Brockton to appear and disrupt her life. That was no different from when she was a kid, waiting for her mother or father to tear her down from the inside out.

Besides the weather, the best part of Arizona was the Knight Family Farm. She'd discovered the family when she first arrived.

Rose and Ben Knight ran a farm with their adult children and their families—a whopping twenty-four point three thousand acres. They operated a quick-service deli featuring their fresh foods. Harlyn ate at the farm daily for lunch and dinner, trying all the different options. Once she tried everything, she repeated her favorites. She never imagined she could eat so healthy on the road. That hadn't always been the case since she left home. She preferred this.

She became friends with Rose and her daughters-in-law, who ran the counter service. They often asked about the bodyguards flanking Harlyn. After the first year, she shared her story. Guilt would have eaten her alive if she hadn't warned them about Brockton and something happened. Thankfully, nothing had.

After getting to know Ben and his boys, they'd been generous with their knowledge, answering all her questions about soil, land, crops, pests, and harvesting—her questions were endless.

"It sounds like you have a love for the earth like we do," Ben declared one day, prompting her to consider a degree in agriculture and working for them.

Over the next several months, she'd taken steps in that direction. She'd gone to the Post Office and rented a mailbox, purchased a laptop, and a phone—she splurged with the newest Apple version. For a week straight, every night, she prayed before lifting her screen and scouring the internet, researching crop science and plant genetics. In the end, she decided on Agronomy, which focused heavily on crop production and soil management. What she'd do with this degree, Harlyn wasn't sure, but she knew that the Spirit filled her with peace the moment she signed up for her first course.

"Here's to my future," Harlyn said, lifting her water bottle in the air. She gulped down half before setting it back on the table. I trust this is your plan, Lord."

She would stay in Arizona on her terms—no more running—explore with an attitude of gratitude and forget everything else.

Chapter 18

A week later, before daybreak, Damon found himself in the butcher shop with Jeff. All the men on the ranch looked to Jeff and Sean for advice as our elders. Sean kept to himself, but the men listened when he spoke. On the other hand, Jeff gave advice away like manna falling from the sky.

"I will give you the best advice that keeps marriages solid," Jeff offered unsolicitedly. "Keep up the PDA. Don't fall victim to the new societal rules. You always hold her hand, drag your hand down her back, hug her, and run your fingers through her hair. Even if your love language isn't touch, it makes a big difference. I promise."

Damon scoffed. "That's excellent advice unless you're married to Harlyn, who instituted a no-touching rule."

He shrugged when Jeff gave him a leery look. "You haven't abandoned that rule yet?"

"I'm trying to be respectful. We're not really married."

"But you are. Your marriage license is legally binding."

Fear gripped Damon's heart. He couldn't be married again. He'd messed it up royally the first time. If he destroyed another marriage, he wouldn't be able to live with himself.

"Maybe you and the Mrs. need to have a candid heart-to-heart," Jeff suggested.

"Perhaps," Damon stated dryly, knowing he wouldn't bring it up any time soon, no matter how much she tempted him.

Jeff threw a chuck of meat into the grinder to produce hamburg. "The best advice I can give you is to make sure the number one thing you have in common is Jesus because that's all that matters. You can have different opinions on anything at all except Jesus."

That's solid advice, for sure. "Thanks, Jeff. I've got to get the kids ready for school."

Damon returned from the butcher shop and greeted Harlyn as she exited the bathroom, leaving him momentarily stunned. Her jeans fit like they were fresh from the dryer, hugging her hips, while her tank top clung to her skin, a staggering sight that left him breathless. The sweatshirt she pulled on next did nothing to erase what he'd already seen.

Needless to say, he was rendered speechless and thankful when Harlyn began speaking, drawing his attention to her lips.

Thankful? Definitely not. More like captivated. It'd been weeks of restless nights sleeping next to Harlyn. The little whimpering and sighing she did in her sleep was pleasant agony.

Finally, he reached her eyes—like bright sunshine, and her long lashes, the rays spreading warmth wherever she looked.

"I left the kids' lunches on the counter with a note for them to have a good day," her sweet voice said, capturing Damon's attention.

"Where are you going?"

"I found a route along Montana Old Highway Ten that seems perfect for autumn photos this morning."

"You can't go off by yourself. It's not safe," he said with as much sincerity as possible.

"This is his M.O. He shows up, and then I don't see him for a year or more."

Harlyn refused to use the dirtbag's name, and for some reason, that felt like a victory to him, causing his chest to soar.

"If he's as evil as you say," she opened her mouth to speak, but Damon continued, "and I'm sure he is; he's planning something for when you least expect it. You have to assume he will change up his ways to catch you off guard."

"Well, I can't live in fear either. I'll only be gone a few hours, and then I'll be back for greenhouse chores."

He knew she was right, but that didn't settle the worriedness creeping into his thoughts.

His phone rang.

"Hey, Quinton." A thought came to him, but he waited patiently to hear why the boss was calling.

"Your groups don't start until one today, correct?"

"Yeah, why?" Harlyn studied him like a textbook before an examination.

Quinton chuckled. "Raddix needs more time off."

That stupid auction. He'd only won because Amelia helped Lily outbid Selena to keep Raddix safe from that villainess. If it hadn't been for that, Damon would have won. He brought in eight hundred dollars from a woman a few towns over.

There is no point in dwelling on what could have been. Since Raddix won, we had to figure out how to get the work covered whenever he asked for time off. He only had until the end of the year with that deal. If Damon were Raddix, he'd probably do the same, so he wouldn't begrudge the man. Besides, it might help Damon out this time, too.

"What needs to be done?"

"Raddix is taking care of the chores with your horses now, and you'll need to help Sean with the end-of-the-day chores."

A smile spread across his face while Harlyn stared at him with skepticism.

"Perfect. I'm taking Harlyn off the ranch, so I'll get the kids ready and drop them at the main house. Is it okay if they sleep on the couch until breakfast?"

"Sure. Talk to you later. Be safe."

"Thanks."

He pocketed his phone and shot her a smile that might win Harlyn that Pultizer.

"I've got to get the kids awake and dressed, or at the very least transported to the main house. Reneé won't care if they do school in their pajamas. Emmanuel lives in his."

He took off down the hallway, opening doors left and right. A tornado of orders flew from his mouth.

"Get up, guys. You can sleep at the main house, but I've got to go somewhere with Harlyn. Brush your teeth, change, or bring clothes if you want to change later, and don't forget your school bags."

"Um." Harlyn trailed behind him. She put her palm on his shoulder. "Settle down. I doubt they heard anything except 'bags' because they're not even awake yet."

He suddenly noticed her hand on his shoulder. Eyeing her long, soft fingers, which Darlene clearly painted with cute blue polish, he smiled and met her gaze.

All he had to do was lean down and feel her tempting lips. Their eyes locked until Dean stumbled out of his room, rubbing the sleep from his eyes. "If you guys are going to do that married stuff, could you do it in your room, please? I need the bathroom."

That married stuff? Damon lost it. He caught his hand on the wall, slightly bent at the waist, laughing with vigor.

"Stop it and let him pass." Harlyn pulled Damon toward the wall, leaving a passable lane in the hall.

"Hey, hands off," Damon teased, raising his eyebrows, letting her know that she once again broke her own rule—the same one Jeff just encouraged him to eliminate. "None of that married stuff in the hall."

Harlyn moved within centimeters of his face. Leaning closer, she whispered. "No touching applies to you." A quick wink and a little pat on his chest were like cherries on top of his favorite sundae.

For the second time that morning, Damon was speechless.

"This is spectacular," Harlyn said as she snapped pictures of the trees donning a sea of colors—gold, red, orange, and yellow. A few stubborn green leaves were still clinging to life, but they, too, would soon meet their destiny.

"It's stunning." Damon's gaze lingered on his wife as she kept her eyes on God's handiwork in the form of trees and the lake that reflected the tower's colorful leaves. He was referring to the beauty next to him, but the moment had passed.

Sadly, he hadn't kissed his wife yet. Jeff had his mind racing about the no-touching rule, and Tanner put thoughts into his head the night they married. "She's a straight shooter. She wouldn't have married you if she didn't have feelings for you, too."

Too? Did Damon have feelings for her? He didn't think so. Yes, her exquisite beauty kicked him in the gut at least once a day, and her kindness was shown through her smile and daily comments. She was considerate. She remembered that hamburgers were his favorite and made them last night. She was doing little things like that often. Her motherly tendencies left him awe-struck every time. Was she just doing her part of the deal, or did she really care about his kids?

Maybe someone might need to explain to the rest of him that he didn't have feelings for her because the memo he'd received was as murky as Yellowstone River after a heavy rain.

"Ready to move along?" Harlyn's sweet voice sounded in his chest, lighting it up like a field of fireflies.

He stepped back, giving her room to close the tripod. He grabbed the structure and shouldered the bag, giving her a nod.

"You don't have to carry everything. I normally do that by myself."

"Now you don't have to."

Harlyn tucked a piece of hair behind her ear. He loved the flush filling her cheeks. Getting her flustered had turned into his favorite activity.

"Here, you can hold this." She turned, eager to grab something. Damon's extended hand waited, wide open, for her to accept the invitation. His heart floundered as the seconds ticked, waiting for her to decide.

When she finally laced her fingers with his, every inch of his skin tingled. *Impossible. I am a man. I don't tingle.*

It was a sting or an annoying itch, but definitely not a tingle.

Despite feeling like a pack mule, Damon relished in whatever this *not-a-tingle* moment meant for them. Sweat started to form under his hat.

"It's been a couple of weeks since our marriage. Is there anything making you regret your decision?" Her soft, hesitant voice pulled at Damon.

He swung their linked arms back and forth. "I'm making some concessions."

"Such as," Harlyn asked in an earnest tone.

"I like keeping the seat up without people yelling at me that they fell in. I like controlling what's on the TV, so I don't have to endure the Bachelor, some other stupid reality show, or commercials." He winked at her, hoping she knew he was playing. "In short, I don't want a woman telling me how to pee or what to watch."

Harlyn's incredulous laugh caused him to tug her hand to a stop. "What's so funny?"

"You are delusional. I've never complained about it, nor have I fallen in the toilet when you left the lid up." Her free hand on her jutted-out hip stole his only available brain cell. "Lastly, I don't do *The Bachelor* or any other reality show."

Getting her all riled up was fun. Cheryl had always gotten so offended when he teased her, but Harlyn just laughed.

She was right. Every night, once Damon turned over, the room lit up from her phone. She'd read for who knows how long. One morning, he woke up, and she was still reading, claiming she had to know how things played out. His heart cried when she said, "I read to escape the misery. I know these are fictional, but it's much better than what I endure in real life."

As the sun rose higher in the sky, the rays reflected off the water, spotlighting the golden tones in Harlyn's hair. He watched her apply lip gloss—another punch in the gut. *How does that lip gloss taste?* He wondered as he studied the slow movement of her hand applying the shiny layer of lip coverage.

Damon shook his head free of any further thoughts about her lips and tugged her along the path, admiring the new season of life God had given him.

In perfect Harlyn style, she spoke whatever was on her mind. "If you could use an emoji to describe our relationship, which would you choose?"

"Seriously?" Damon hoped he masked his shock. Leave it to Harlyn to ask him something he'd never think of on his own.

"Maybe the one with the open mouth, wide eyes, and hands on its cheeks, like the kid from *Home Alone*."

Harlyn's sweet laughter echoed across the pond, striking him in the chest. He wasn't sure how much longer he could keep his feelings bottled up.

"What is your one guilty pleasure?" Damon wondered aloud.

"I only get one?"

Damon's face burned. Somehow, his mind read way farther into her response. "Y-yep."

"Ice cream or chips," Harlyn admitted.

"Any particular flavors?"

"Mint Chocolate Chip and Cool Ranch Doritos."

"Good to know."

"My turn." Harlyn had a little hop to her step, making Damon smile at her carefree attitude. "What do you spend the most time thinking about and why?"

You as of late. He definitely wasn't admitting that. He must have stronger feelings for Harlyn than she did him, and he wouldn't make this situation any more uncomfortable than necessary, especially since the whole being married thing still set his nerves ablaze.

"My kiddos, of course, but my horses are a close second, and the groups I work with make up much of my thinking."

They walked along in a comfortable silence, his mind racing, wondering what she was thinking. Then, it hit him, and his eyes widened before he could stop.

His heart lurched, and he drew a sharp breath. Fear pricked the base of his spine. Jeff had been right.

He was falling for his wife.

Chapter 19

The month-long heat wave had kept Harlyn mainly in her motorhome with the AC on, looking for the rest of her freedom. Grandpa was the ultimate hide-and-seek gamer. She'd looked on and off for the last eight years and hadn't found it. Whatever *it* was, Harlyn wasn't exactly sure, but she knew God would put it in her path when the time was right.

"Grandpa, what am I looking for?" Harlyn hollered into the sky as she exited her motorhome. She ground her teeth together.

Although the songbird's melodic tune in reply was beautiful, it wasn't the answer Harlyn was looking for. She plopped down in her oversized camping chair, granting the sun permission to fill her with Vitamin D.

Not finding whatever she was looking for was only part of her frustration. Harlyn had earned her Bachelor of Science in Agronomy, hoping to work for the Knight Family. Sadly, hard times hit them like everyone else, and they couldn't hire anyone outside of the family at the time.

They didn't know Halryn's financial standing, so when she offered to work for free to practice everything she'd just learned, Ben refused, saying it wasn't right to take advantage of such a good customer and friend.

Harlyn decided to help them out in other ways. She continued to eat at the farm daily and tip them generously.

Spending the last eight years alone (besides six impressive bodyguards) was a blessing and a curse. Her ability to move around the country and live how she wanted was a gift from God. She'd gone whitewater rafting, on a hot air balloon ride, hiked through nearly all of central Arizona, and even gone to college—online, but that was only semantics. She still couldn't believe she had a degree. It seemed kind of useless without the Knight Farm.

Then again, she frequently heard *Be still* or *let us run with perseverance the race marked out for us.* Who was Harlyn to argue with God's word? No one. So she soldiered on. Now she'd returned to patiently, not so patiently, wait. For what? Heck, if she knew.

She crumbled inside when she let herself think too much about being alone forever or not finding whatever Grandpa planted for her. While in school, she was distracted and didn't think about whatever hidden treasure would contribute to her freedom. Now, without the distraction and hearing, *"Be still"* from the Lord, she had to work hard not to plunge into despair whenever those words rang through her head.

There'd been a brief season when she thought she and Mike, her former bodyguard, might try to move beyond their professional relationship.

They both enjoyed the same music, being outdoors, and helping others. But in the end, his desire to protect the rich and famous took precedence in his life. The renowned aspect most likely appealed to him since Harlyn was rich enough to buy a small country. Not that she ever flaunted it, but she did wonder, briefly, why she wasn't good enough for Mike. Harlyn didn't begrudge him. It was fun while it lasted. Since then, her heart ached, constantly wondering if she'd ever have a chance at love.

"All right, that's enough of that." Harlyn hopped out of the chair, wiped the mist from her eyes, and returned to the AC.

Her eyes scanned her motorhome. "I have to find whatever Grandpa left for me and start a real life."

She rested on her knees in front of one of the storage cabinets. She would pull each one apart until she found something or cleared the area.

Harlyn didn't want to live in her house on wheels any longer. She wanted a home on a foundation, a backyard, a child or two, and maybe even a dog. Could she ever find anyone willing to put up with her past? Her Grandpa's words came back to her. *"God is preparing the right man for you."* Hopefully, she wouldn't be elderly by the time the preparations were finished.

Several hours later, Harlyn was on the last cabinet in the main area. Her feet were tingly and numb from sitting on her knees, rummaging through the cupboards, and pulling everything out, including the bottoms. Nothing. *What the heck am I looking for?*

She plopped down on her rear, resting her elbows on her knees, and dropped her forehead into her palms. If she could just talk to her Grandpa one more time, would he tell her anything now?

With tired hands, she lifted the bottom part of the cabinet floor. A shiny metal box sat there lonely. Finally, all would be revealed. Her hunt for freedom was over.

Pulling the box onto her lap, she attempted to lift the silver flap over the keyhole. Locked. Of course, she didn't expect anything else. Tugging the chain from around her neck, she palmed the key. Fingers trembling, Harlyn lined up the key with the hole in the box. She slid the key in. Her heart raced with excitement. *Finally, I'll know what my Grandparents have been eluding to all my life.* She turned the key, but her hand slipped. The key remained still as a stone. Haryln's heart sank quicker than an anchor to the ocean floor.

Doubt ebbed and flowed throughout her life just like anyone else's, but now her doubt felt more like a tumultuous ocean storm. Like sea waves and winds violently tossing her back and forth.

Before she could slip into any further despair, Harlyn closed her eyes and prayed. "Thank you, Lord, for blessing me. Heck, I must be the most blessed person in the world." She'd read in the book of James that morning, *"Blessed is the man who perseveres under trial."*

"My whole life has been a trial, Lord! But I know you are still here because you keep giving me that faith. Thank you. I don't want to imagine my life without you in it. I trust you. If you want me to leave here, tell me. I will follow you, Amen."

"Harlyn."

"Yeah," she jumped, turning toward Jet, one of her bodyguards from the second group. "Sorry, you scared me."

"Sorry." His serious tone revealed his words were more routine than authentic. "Do you think it's time we left Arizona?"

"No." she didn't hesitate. "I am not running anymore. When I get good and ready to leave Arizona, we will." Her words were sharp, but her tone was casual.

Jet crossed his bulky arms over his chest.

Mocking him with her stance, Harlyn raised her eyebrows, challenging him further.

"Are we really doing this again?"

"Apparently," Harlyn snipped. "I'm not trying to be difficult. I can only imagine how difficult your job is, but I won't let *him,* she didn't want that vermin's name on her lips, chase me out of Arizona until the Lord tells me to leave."

"I appreciate your dedication to the Lord, but it's our job to ensure you're safe, and we'd all like to go home to our wives alive."

Ouch. Harlyn already felt bad enough, keeping these men away from their families. The last time she'd spoken with Richard and Stan, they both recommended keeping the bodyguards since Brockton hadn't squelched his efforts of following her.

"You're free to leave any time," Harlyn wouldn't back down to anyone.

Her mind drifted. Two months ago, Brockton followed her through the Botanical Gardens. He gripped her wrist when she moved to a more secluded part of the path. Instantly, Jet had his meaty hand on Brockton's meek shoulder, crippling him.

"Let go of the lady. Now!"

Harlyn got in Brockton's face. "We don't have a future. Go home and leave me alone."

"You are coming home with me one way or another. We will marry, and I'll be set for life."

Something in her snapped. Harlyn slapped him so hard his head whipped to the side. Before her punch coming from the other hand could swing his head in the other direction, Karl, the youngest of her bodyguards, appeared, wrapping his hand around her waist and holding her arm back. Lifting her off the ground and out of the situation, she hollered for him to put her down. Jet told her later that Brockton threatened to press charges. Jet encouraged him to do so, as it would be deemed self-defensive given the grip marks on Harlyn's wrist that eventually disappeared days later. Her photography skills and tripod came in handy that day, but she gave the prints and digital copies to Richard, not wanting to see them again.

"We're not leaving you unless you fire us."

"Do you want me to fire you?"

"Not really. This is a cushy job, relatively speaking, but your feistiness gets us concerned sometimes." She didn't take offense. These guys could be forced into real danger with guns blazing and bullets flying. Dealing with Brockton was more of a nuisance than anything.

"I'll work on toning it down a notch. But we're still not leaving here. Not yet."

"Okay."

"Now, can you please help me open this box?"

Chapter 20

What a day! She and Damon spent the entire morning together, taking pictures, talking, and holding hands. Yes, she broke her own *'no touching'* rule, and it felt magnificent.

As quickly as that feeling came, it disappeared with lightspeed. He still carried her equipment, but any gentleman would. Her cold hand yearned for his warmth, but it never came. *What happened?* One minute, he extended his hand, and the next, his expression looked more torturous than happy. Damon opened her door, cupping her elbow. He'd ensured she made it safely into his truck, but it felt robotic, almost out of duty or expectation, not fluid.

By the time they returned to the ranch, they weren't even speaking, and for the first time, Harlyn was too self-conscious to say anything.

Damon focused on the animals, and Harlyn headed for the greenhouses. Nurturing plants brought her a sense of peace that she appreciated, but her mind raced with thoughts. *What did I say or do to upset him? Is he mad? Did his quietness even have anything to do with me? Is he missing his ex-wife? Ouch! That one hurt the most. Had they had any contact over the years?* She didn't want to know.

Once she finished her work, she checked in with Amelia and Quinton to see if they needed her help with anything else.

"That's really nice to offer," Quinton began. "Do you have any other skills that would be useful on a ranch?"

"Quinton!" Amelia barked, causing Quinton and Harlyn's heads to snap in her direction.

"What?"

"That was insulting."

"I didn't take offense to the question. It was legitimate, considering he's the foreman and me the employee. He needs to know how I can be most useful."

Quinton kissed Amelia's temple. "She tends to be a little sensitive but has grown so much since I met her." He winked at his wife, filling Harlyn with an ache, wondering what it would take for Damon to look at her like that.

In the end, they determined she didn't have many useful skills to help out independently, so Quinton sent her to the horse corral to help Damon manage the kids.

Damon's second group had started just moments before she'd arrived. Based on his tight-lipped smile, Quinton must have already told Damon she was there to help him out.

What had she done?

"Kiddos, sit up straight in the saddle and tighten your stomach muscles."

Of course, it made sense for Damon to be shirtless for modeling purposes. When he tightened his core muscles, showcasing every abdominal muscle he had, ones she hadn't even known existed, she sucked in a hard breath, and the skin on her face scorched, exposing truths, she wasn't ready to share.

"Are you okay?" Damon asked with an amused tone.

"Yep, just fine." She gravitated toward Emmanuel, hoping to skip over this moment.

Emmanuel blared, "Yeah, Harlyn, you look sick."

Lovesick, maybe. "I'm good, Emmanuel. Let's focus on helping you. Can you make your back straighter?"

"Yeah, but if you're going to throw up, don't do it on me."

Damon sniggered, frustrating her even more.

The hour zoomed by, and Damon was off to milk the cows for Raddix. Quinton joined Harlyn in the barn and taught her how to take the saddles off the horses and brush them down.

"Thanks for your willingness to learn and help out. You'll fit in perfectly around here," Quinton stated.

Harlyn acknowledged him with a smile, not feeling at all content. She had half a mind to stalk over to the milking barn and force Damon to explain himself.

Fortunately, she let that scenario play out in her mind and decided against it. She could read the caption now: Crazy *fake* wife harassed *fake* husband because he wasn't expressing himself. There must be a slew of videos (like blooper reels on steroids) dealing with that topic on social media, not that she spent time on those sites, fearing her parents or Brockton would find her. It didn't matter; somehow, they always knew her whereabouts.

This was definitely not her typical way of handling things. She only ran away from her parents and Brockton because she believed danger was imminent. Damon didn't pose a physical danger, only an emotional one.

"She's too perfect." A man's voice echoed through the barn, and Harlyn froze. The familiar-sounding voice produced bumps on her skin, and her heart leaped.

"I tried to tell you," Tanner's voice followed.

"Don't put any more ideas in my head. Our marriage—it's only a means to an end."

The faintness of his voice made her question whether she heard him correctly. When Quinton asked if she was okay, she knew she had, and her heart spilled on the barn floor.

"I'm good," she muttered quietly.

Her phone buzzed. Damon must be texting to remind her that she promised him and the kids she'd make lasagna, her specialty.

Adding grief to her already injured heart, she read Damon's text.

> I'm heading to the dance hall with Tanner. I already said good night to the kids. See you later if you're still awake.

She could read between the lines—*don't wait up. I'll be busy tonight.* She mocked in the best Damon tone she could muster in her head.

Harlyn wouldn't let his words affect her. If only she could erase Damon's words from her brain or rip off her ears, preventing her from ever hearing him say that in the first place, but she couldn't.

She did what any self-respecting wife would do. Her thumbs flew over the keyboard on her phone.

> Whatever.

She stuffed her phone back in her pocket. Harlyn wanted to storm up to him and demand he explain himself, but again, she remembered this was only a fake arrangement. Nonetheless, she'd make him give her answers when he got home.

Perhaps his distance and her inner doubt were due to the tension surrounding her *'no touching'* rule. She hadn't been real strict with it—they'd held hands or brushed shoulders, but it had become their private joke. Her insides clenched, thinking about having an inside joke with Damon.

The other night was a missed opportunity to change the rule, and she'd been kicking herself, figuratively speaking, ever since. Damon graced her shoulder when he got into bed, leaving pins and needles in his wake. Her lungs ceased, but she'd played it off as a sigh one might make in their sleep when she reminded herself to breathe.

Fake marriage, fake sleeping, what's next? Harlyn hated that her feelings were obviously a lot stronger than Damon's since touching each other didn't have the same effect on him as it did on her. She didn't want to make a fool of herself, and sleeping was usually her best chance to avoid mishaps.

Harlyn finished with the horses and thanked Quinton for his help.

"Are you and the kids having dinner at the main house?"

She smiled as she watched them play tag. Even Dean and Charlotte, Reneé and Rocco's oldest, joined the younger kids.

"Thank you, but no. I promised them lasagna, so if you don't need my help anymore, I'll go wash up and start dinner. Then, I'll come back and get them when it's baking."

"Sounds good."

An hour later, the kid's praise for her food lifted her spirits. "Dad doesn't know what he missed tonight." Dean rinsed his plate and set it in the dishwasher. Harlyn shared that their dad was out with Uncle Tanner, but they made the best of the evening.

Two hours and two card games later, the kids were finally in bed. She wasn't surprised that the kids teamed up against her in Apples to Apples, but she whipped their butts at Skip-Bo.

Harlyn was cozy in bed, reading Kimberly Krey's newest book in her cowboy series. As expected, the kisses were steamy, causing Harlyn's mind to shift to Damon. The heavens above were against Harlyn or for her, depending on one's perspective.

The book sucked Harlyn in. With every turned page, she heard the coyotes howl. Those howls became clearer and more intense, matching Harlyn's emotions.

By the time she finished the book, Damon still hadn't arrived home. He'd pay for it tomorrow since he was up with the rooster. Had she done something so awful that he couldn't even stand being in the same house, his house, with her?

Though she'd read a book to distract her from her own crazy life, now that she'd finished, her mind scrambled around like a child trying to capture a muddy piglet at a rodeo.

She needed to end this charade tonight. It wasn't fair that Damon didn't even want to be in his own house or with his children.

Harlyn wasn't sure what she'd do. Obviously, she'd stay clear of the East Coast, but she'd free Damon of his misery when he got home.

She learned long ago that once her grandparents died, she didn't have anyone else left in her corner. She'd been on her own long enough. She'd rather be alone than deal with manipulating and controlling people ever again.

Chapter 21

"You can't be serious, Tan." Damon slammed his glass down on the table, capturing the attention of the surrounding tables.

"I'm tired. How many Gold Buckles does one need?"

Damon leaned back, crossing his arms over his chest. "If I recall, your own words when I first met you, *'One Gold Buckle isn't enough; heck, a million wouldn't be enough for me.'*"

An all too confident smile spread across Damon's face.

"I knew you'd remember those words." Tanner chugged his drink, emptying his glass. "I want the sweet wife who loves me for me. I won't complain if I have a horse or two, a dog, two or three kids, you know, the works."

He knew all too well what that felt like. Once with Cheryl, he'd thought he had the picture-perfect, white picket fence life. That blew up in his hands like a grenade, with shrapnel still lodged in his heart.

Then, a beautiful redhead grabbed his attention at the festival. Even now, as a blonde, Harlyn had taken up permanent residency in his mind. In the weeks since, he'd felt his attraction to Harlyn in the pit of his stomach and the walls of his narrow esophagus.

He'd told Cheryl that he loved her first. Not that he was anywhere ready to say that to Harlyn, but it was the reminder he needed not to make the mistake a second time. Maybe it wasn't fair of him to think Harlyn would be like Cheryl, but everyone knows what they say about one spoiled apple.

"Excuse me," a voluptuous brunette stood between Damon and Tanner. "Are you Tanner Brooks?" The first Buckle Bunnies' eager, seductive tone caused Damon to chuckle, thanking God they were after his buddy and not him.

Tanner tipped the brim of his hat. "Yes, I am, Darlin', but tonight I'm here with my buddy, Gold Buckle winner Damon Richards."

"Oh, you're a cowboy, too." Buckle Bunny number two—blonde and just as endowed as Buckle Bunny number one—snuggled up to Damon. Her friend was practically sitting on Tanner's lap, and he hung off the other end.

"No. I just wear the hat and boots to trick bunnies like you." Damon didn't know where that'd come from, but she was put off enough to stop caressing his shoulder and bicep long enough to think about what he'd said.

When Tanner burst out laughing, so did both the women. Damon loved how Harlyn laughed at herself when she did something silly or when a frog invaded her space. These women didn't have a clue that they were laughing at themselves.

"I'm married, so if—"

Someone shoved on his free side, cutting off his words. The music screeched to a stop when Damon and Tanner pushed their chairs back, ready for whatever would come next.

"What's your problem?" they asked at the same time.

A sinister smile crept across this grotesquely huge man's face, and veins protruded from each arm like Twizzlers in a checkout line.

Three men about half his size but still big enough to give Tanner and Damon a good fight were situated on both sides of the man.

"You're Damon Richards, right?" The monstrous goon asked.

"Yeah, so. Who are you?" Damon's grumpy persona shone. He didn't care about those bunnies still lingering or the goons. He wanted to be left alone.

His thoughts had distracted him a second too long. Despite Tanner's warning and his best effort to move or duck, the man cold-clocked Damon in the jaw.

It hurt, but not as much as Damon had thought a punch from those tree trunks would. He motioned for the women to move further away than they had. The tables on every side of them were now vacant. Damon rubbed his jaw, spit a mouthful of blood into his glass, looked at Tanner, and said, "This could mess up your last ride."

"I'm all in for you, buddy."

That was all Damon needed to hear before their fist were flying.

Sheriff McDugal and Deputy Williams were not happy with them. Williams was on duty, so he had to respond. Due to the nature of the incident, he needed Sheriff McDugal's assistance.

Raddix and McDugal had gone to school together a couple of years apart. He seemed to be a good guy, coming to the rescue when a stalker had Raddix's wife, Lily, tied to a chair, waving a gun at her a couple of months back.

Damon didn't get that sheriff. He got the you-just-woke-me-up-at-this-hour, madder than Mt. St. Helen when she erupted over forty years ago, sheriff.

Fortunately, the anger was directed at the three goons Brockton likely hired to eliminate Damon. With him out of the picture, Brockton probably thought he could sweep in and take Harlyn back to her prison life—not today, not ever. Over his dead body were his exact thoughts.

Damon chose to press charges. Whether this was seen as simple battery, a misdemeanor, aggravated battery (which it should be), or a felony, Damon wouldn't let these thugs, Brockton or Harlyn's parents think they could bully anyone from Haven Ridge.

Once the three thugs were cuffed and in the back of Deputy Williams's squad car, looking like Bluto, Olive Oil, and Popeye without his spinach,

Sheriff McDugal chatted with Damon and Tanner while the establishment owner gave the two men ice for their knuckles.

Damon caught the sheriff's gaze drifting. A quick glimpse revealed a blonde with perfectly adorn hair. Willow Payne was Damon's ticket out of a verbal lashing. Gerard shuffled his feet, obviously itching to see his favorite hairdresser. His hands rapped against his thighs. *Maybe all the rumors about the sheriff's feelings for the pastor's daughter are true?*

"If you're all set, fellas, I'll make a quick stop . . ." he tilted his head toward Willow, "and then head back home. No more trouble, okay?"

"Sure thing." Damon hated it when people said things like that to the victim as if he'd attacked them. Everyone knew he hadn't or he'd be at the station right now, but Gerard wasn't thinking clearly.

Tanner walked away from the brawl with a cut lip and a bruised ego, "I'll feel that tomorrow."

"Fortunately, the Nationals aren't until December. Do you plan on staying at the ranch until then?"

"Yeah. In fact, I've already talked to Amelia and Quinton about returning after I win and working for them."

"Seriously? Where are you going to work if you don't win?" Damon picked up his phone and texted Quinton to tell him what happened.

"Hardy-Har-Har." Tanner punched Damon's shoulder, but Damon didn't even flinch.

His phone pinged with a text from Quinton.

Everything okay now?

Yes.

Let Rohan know that we'll take care of the damages right now. Don't want him waiting for the money—courts take a long time. Tell him to send us a bill.

Will do.

Damon rubbed the heel of his palms into his eyes. "Great, you're staying on at the ranch. That means I can go home and get some shut-eye because you'll be around so much I'll get sick of you."

"Teasing again? Harlyn is good for you. I can't remember when you ever attempted to have a sense of humor."

As the men left, they thanked the owner, and Damon relayed Quinton's message, which Rohan was super grateful for—much to Damon's chagrin—the man even hugged him.

Damon already had a massive black and blue mark on his jaw. When he got home, he hoped Harlyn was sleeping. The last thing he wanted to do was have *the talk*.

Chapter 22

Harlyn, perched against the headboard with her arms crossed, glared at Damon as he stumbled through the dark, gathering his shorts and t-shirt for bed.

Damon glanced toward the bed as if he could feel her stare. "Harlyn?" His voice broke.

She wouldn't pretend to be asleep again tonight. No Siree. She wanted answers.

He'd already made it unscathed through the pitch-black house to the bedroom despite her making sure every light was off at the stroke of midnight. It was time to cast light upon their situation.

Harlyn flicked the switch on the wall by the bed, illuminating the room. She bit back a smile when Damon jumped. "Do you know what time it is?"

Great job; you will definitely be known as the crazy fake wife before the evening is over.

Before Damon could say anything, she bolted out of bed, rushing to his side, forgetting her anger. "Are you okay? What happened?"

"I-I." Damon sputtered.

Great, he doesn't want to tell me. Whatever took place must have involved a woman. He smells like a woman. What'd he do, hit on some man's wife?

"Never mind. It's none of my business. I shouldn't have asked," Harlyn spit out.

A tsunami of jealousy crashed down on her, and she hated it. She knew this was a fake marriage. He'd already put himself out there to protect her from Brockton. It wasn't fair of her to expect more of him. But if he was out hitting on other women, how believable of a couple were they? She refused to mention that she was drowning in the murky waters of jealousy.

"You're jumping to conclusions."

Harlyn let out a big sigh. "I'm sorry. I know this situation came out of nowhere, and our marriage, sorry, fake marriage is just a means to an end."

His eyes bugged out. "How do you keep hearing only the parts of my conversations with people that make me look bad?"

She shrugged, gripping her midsection for support. Harlyn never let him tell her how he got the mark on his jaw. It was too late to backtrack now.

Remembering the reason for her irritation, she sprung ahead with the momentum of a swimmer breaking the surface from ten feet down.

"I've been quiet but can't do it anymore." His handsome face, etched with confusion, encouraged her to continue. "You know, training Meadow after your work day ends and heading to the dance hall with Tanner just to avoid me."

Meanwhile, she completed her greenhouse expectations without him, even though he was supposed to be guiding her along—not that she needed the help—but the overwhelming desire to be around him, to have a real future with him and the kids, grew like wildflowers through her soul.

At that moment, Damon ran his hand through his hair. *Look away.* It was definitely not the time to be enamored with him.

Her hands now gripped her hips, and her voice raised an octave, still mindful of sleeping children. "The kids missed you."

She hated mentioning the kids because she enjoyed spending time with them, and being there for them was part of their deal, but she could tell they wanted their dad, too.

"Are they the only ones who missed me?" Amusement filled his face as the corners of his mouth lifted ever so slightly.

Harlyn sucked in a ragged breath, and her cheeks were warming by the nanosecond. *I should have pretended to sleep.*

Recovering relatively quickly, she replied, "I'm sure Black Jack, Apple Jack, and Blaze want more of your time, too."

His full smile accentuated his cute dimples and dried her throat. She'd never seen those, probably because Mr. Serious had never given her an authentic smile.

Damon caught her gaze once she finally stopped examining his handsome facial features as if he were the main attraction on the evening menu. "I have a very good reason for going out with Tanner."

Harlyn waited. And we waited. And waited some more.

"Does it have anything to do with why you stopped talking to me this morning after we took pictures together?"

A hint of admission shone in his eyes. Then, he did the unthinkable. Damon stepped closer, his gaze never leaving hers. His milk chocolate eyes turned darker, making her throat constrict. His calloused fingers, rough against her soft skin, brushed over her collarbone, pushing her hair off her shoulder.

He was going to kiss her. He leaned in, stopping an inch in front of her lips. *Thank you, God. Finally!* His heated breath sent a cast of hawk's wings flapping in her low belly. *Come on, kiss me. What was he thinking?* Harlyn was so confused.

She'd worked so hard to stay hidden from her parents and Brockton that she never even thought about becoming romantic with anyone. Now, to be free from them, she'd married a man who convinced her that she wanted a real marriage—with him. If he had communicated more, she would know what he was thinking. Could she kiss him and risk falling even deeper?

"Is it hot in here?" Harlyn bursts out, feeling naked and exposed.

By the time she'd stepped back, her breath labored, her throat now sandpaper, and her lips ached for a kiss. He was playing his husband role a little *too well*.

Harlyn snapped, "You know, Damon, just because you don't try to control people doesn't mean you don't hurt them. Her voice trembled with sadness. "In fact, you're a bigger jerk than Brockton."

"Excuse me," he balked as if she'd slapped him.

"Pretending to care for someone and then blowing them off is so much worse." She lifted her finger. Thankfully, she didn't poke it into his chest. He told her that Cheryl used to do that, and it annoyed him. "If Brockton is a jerk, then you're a dirtbag."

He stared at her, his eyes flaming fireballs. To avoid eye contact, she stocked back to the bed,

"Why are you so upset?" Damon asked earnestly.

In the back of Harlyn's mind, she thought she might be overreacting, but she couldn't stop her emotions.

Before she could answer, Damon continued. "Furthermore. If anyone is using anyone, it's you using me."

Harlyn whipped around, her hair making a full three-sixty, slapping her in the face.

"Me? You're the one who said we were married."

"To help you!"

He wasn't wrong.

"If you're out galavanting with your buddy, it's hard to convince people you're newly married."

Damon's voice returned to his low, incredibly alluring tone. "Ah. I see the problem. You're jealous. I bet when you said no touching, you didn't really mean it."

Not wrong again. Sort of. She meant it at the time. But with each passing day, she wished she'd never said that. She imagined if Damon held and comforted her, she'd feel amazing.

He was a panther inching his way toward Harlyn. "Maybe you did mean it, but after sharing a bed with me, your resolve is weakening and—"

"—You are so off base," Harlyn interrupted, hoping her voice held firm.

Still gliding his way toward her, Harlyn backed up, but she ran out of the room.

"You still haven't told me why you've been avoiding me." Harlyn squeaked out.

"It's complicated. I need some more time before I explain."

Harlyn grabbed his pillow and shoved it into his chest. "No problem. Until you figure it out, you can sleep on the couch."

His mouth dropped. "What?!"

"You heard me," she said, tossing his quilt at him too.

"Our marriage is fake, pretend, a sham, but this," he pointed to his bed, "is real and mine."

She pushed out an oh-dear-boy-you-are-sadly-mistaken laugh. "See, we were legally married here in Montana, and in your kids' eyes. Since you messed up big time, you're couch surfing until you fix it."

"I can't believe I'm getting kicked out of my own bed," he muttered on his way out the door.

Damon tried to redeem himself. "I get it. You're mad at me right now, and I'm sorry."

Harlyn's eyes pinned him down. "Until you can tell me exactly what you are sorry for, you're on the couch."

"Fine." He gripped his pillow tighter. "You won this round, but mark my words, you'll beg me to return to bed tomorrow evening."

"Will I?"

"Most definitely."

"Challenge accepted. Goodnight." She wiggled her fingers at him.

The longing look on his face made Harlyn wonder if he wanted to kiss each of her fingers as much as she wanted him to.

"Oh, Damon?"

"Yes," his voice hopeful.

"Turn out the light before you go, please."

He swiped his fingers down the switch with more force than necessary, letting her know he was frustrated.

"Thank you."

"Don't mention it," he huffed.

Chapter 23

"That stubborn woman is getting the best of me," Damon complained to Tanner and Raddix the following day. "This morning, she walked around singing that country about the girl besting the guy, and all he has is his guitar."

"Ah, Luke Combs," Tanner raved. "Good guy. I met him at NPR last year. He's a huge bronc riding fan."

Shoving the pitchfork more aggressively than necessary into the hay, Damon continued. "Can you believe I had to sleep on my own couch? I had the pleasure of waking up to Dean tsking me. 'What could you have possibly done wrong already, Dad?' he questioned me."

Tanner and Raddix didn't bother to contain their guttural laughs.

"You have it bad, my friend," Raddix said, slapping him on the back.

"Shut up!" Damon bellowed, glaring at Raddix. Harlyn drove him crazy in a good way, and there wasn't anything he could do about it.

"As soon as you have an honest conversation and tell her how you feel instead of hiding out in the dance hall with me, you'll fair much better, I imagine."

"Agreed," Raddix offered his two cents.

"That's what she said." *How can I tell her that I have real feelings for her? What if she doesn't reciprocate?*

"You whoo!"

"Ugh," Raddix and Damon said in unison.

"What's the problem?" Tanner inquired.

Before they could answer, Selena appeared in the doorway.

"Hello, gentlemen." Selena sashayed toward Tanner.

"New meat," Raddix spoke specifically to Damon.

But Tanner questioned, "Who, me?"

"Hi, I'm Selena." She stopped millimeters away from Tanner, placing her thin fingers on his forearm.

"Also known as cowgirl Barbie," Raddix grumbled.

Selena's school-girl chuckle was disgusting. She obviously hadn't changed since she'd admitted to almost running Lily and Raddix off the road. She claimed she wanted Raddix back, but that was never true. Selena was a narcissist who'd lost the control she had over Amelia and others within

Haven Ridge, and she struggled to function. She'd lost Quinton to Amelia and Raddix to Lily.

"Oh, Raddix, you're not still sore about me breaking up with you way back in high school, are you?"

Damon held his forearm across Raddix's heaving chest, preventing him from moving closer to the vixen.

"Your delusional state requires a trip to the nearest mental health facility. Tanner, stay clear of her, or she'll chew you up and spit you out."

"Alright." Damon put his hands up. "What did you come here for, Selena?"

Ignoring Damon, she left her hand attached to Tanner. "I'm looking for Quinton to discuss our trading agreement."

"He's probably hiding from you," Raddix murmured.

"Raddix, quiet!" Damon said with authority. This was harder than getting his children to behave.

"Lily would not be happy with how you're acting toward me," Selena continued to goad Raddix.

Raddix opened his mouth to speak, but Damon interrupted. "Look, Selena, I'll let Quinton know you need to talk to him," Damon declared.

Clearly not getting the hint that she was being dismissed, Selena focused her attention back on Tanner.

"Maybe we could go to the dance hall tonight and get to know each other."

"Drop the act, Selena. No one is buying it," Raddix hissed.

Continuing to gaze at Tanner, Selena responded breathily, "I'm not sure what you mean."

"Let's go, Tanner. We have plans for the evening that don't include serpents," Raddix said, pulling Tanner from Selena's clutches and dragging him from the barn.

"Well, I never," Selena huffed, then turned her attention back to Damon.

"Look, you have to understand how Raddix feels. You tried to kill his wife."

"Wife?"

"Yes, they were married a couple of weeks ago," Damon confirmed, though he believed she already knew.

"I'm going to be alone forever." Selena started sniffling.

Damon wasn't prepared for this side of this foe. "Don't cry. You brought all of your trouble on yourself," he barked impatiently.

Selena was the queen of getting what she wanted by any means necessary, so this crying show was probably a facade, one he didn't have time or energy for.

But then, he remembered something Lily had said multiple times without actually revealing anything specific. "*You never know what someone is dealing with, but it usually explains their behavior.*"

He could apply that thought to himself. It might be his stiff back from sleeping on the couch, making him grumpier this morning than he had been in a while. More than likely, his mood had everything to do with a certain fiery redhead swirling through his mind. That's it. He knew his lack of time with her was responsible for his grumpy mood.

Mustering up his most patient tone, Damon quickly pushed out his next words.

"Selena, if you just be kind and not try to deceive people, you could have a whole town behind you and many friendships."

"Tsk!" Selena's disbelief was evident. "No one in this town would ever give me another chance. Everyone here has even turned the new woman, your fake wife, Harlyn, against me.." Her words dripped with bane. "Speaking of deceiving people. . . " Selena let her words drop off and set in Damon's mind.

The growing feelings of attraction and protection were all too familiar in Damon's chest just at the mere mention of Harlyn's name.

"It'd be an awful shame if someone let it slip you two only married to keep that hunk of a man, Brockton, from being able to marry her." Selena's icy smile filled her face. "From what I hear, the man is quite the charmer—"

"—Yeah, he reminds me of you. Perhaps we should introduce the two of you."

Damon had once thought that he wouldn't wish Brockton and Harlyn's parents on his worst enemy, but maybe he was wrong.

"Nah, I'd rather see him get with the woman he was promised."

Now, it was Damon's turn to see red. He was an indulgent man unless someone messed with his family.

"This is why no one wants you around. You're so filled with malice that people don't trust you!"

His unyielding eyes bore into her. "I've never dealt with your evilness directly, but I promise you'll regret it if you do anything to disrupt my family."

At the speed of light, her tears halted. She puffed her chest out and stood ramrod straight, trying to make herself appear bigger. "I don't take kindly to threats, so you, Sir, should probably know I'll do whatever helps me the most."

"Get out of my barn!" Damon roared. Apple Jack and Black Jack neighed loudly, and their nostrils flared. Damon turned his attention to them just as Raddix and Tanner returned.

"Everything okay in here?"

"No. Selena was just leaving and not returning unless someone invited her."

Selena flicked her hair over her shoulder. It would have smacked Damon in the face had he not moved.

"That woman is pure evil." Damon stalked out of the barn toward the main house.

***

Three long days had passed since his encounter with Selena. Damon hated complaining, but Amelia had asked what happened when she saw him ready to erupt. Thankfully, she stepped in to deal with Selena. From now on, either she or Katy would bring Selena's order to her dad's ranch and pick up their eggs at that time, eliminating the need for Selena to step foot back on the ranch.

"Had I known all it would take to get rid of Selena was ticking you off, I would have made that happen years ago," Raddix let out a breath of a laugh.

"Funny."

"Don't worry about her. It's her word against the ours and the sheriff's. We've got yours and Harlyn's backs."

"Thanks, Man."

It wasn't like Brockton could do anything anyway. Their marriage was legal; they just started it unconventionally.

Damon said good night to Meadow and flicked off the lights as he exited the barn, holding the door for Raddix.

The sky-blue backdrop slowly melted away as the golden light rested on the horizon, bidding farewell to the day's brilliant sun and its warmth. He was suddenly aware of Harlyn and Darlene strolling toward the main house hand in hand, with the boys behind them shoving each other.

His heart galloped at Harlyn's rare but unmistakably bright smile—the one he saw the night they played outside with his kids.

All three of his children donned sweatshirts, which he knew was all Harlyn's doing. He wondered how much of a fight they put up with her to wear one.

She still hadn't given in and let Damon back in bed. Undoubtedly, she would stick to her word until he told her what was happening with him.

"Stubborn woman," Damon mumbled.

The cackle behind him reminded him that he wasn't alone. "How's the couch treating you?" Raddix slapped him on the back.

Harlyn had more to lose than him, but that didn't seem to matter in her eyes.

A fiery spark lit his core. Harlyn's determination to stick up for herself was so dang attractive. Unfortunately, he was the one she was going against.

"I haven't gone out since that night, and she still won't let me sleep in my own bed." Damon scoffed.

"Maybe you going out wasn't the problem."

Warmth filled Damon's chest as he watched his kids and Harlyn enjoying the simple task of walking on the ranch. That was what he'd wanted all along.

There'd been a time when he'd thought Cheryl completed him—kids, love, friendship. Sadly, he'd only gotten a third of the deal. Arguably, the kids were the best part of the deal. *Was it too much to want it all?*

Seeing Darlene and the boys connect with Harlyn so quickly made him wonder if God had sent Harlyn to the ranch to complete his little family.

"Daddy!" Darlene bolted to and jumped in Damon's arms. "Harlyn is the greatest. She's played with me since school got out. Well, we had to do the laundry and clean up, too. The boys grumbled about it, but they did it." Her face beamed. "We hung the pictures up on the wall that she took."

His gaze followed Harlyn to the group that'd just arrived for a game of Manhunt. It amazed Damon that Harlyn, in a thick sweatshirt and jeans, could get his blood racing.

"Hey, Dad," Dean waved his hands in front of Damon's face. "Dad!"

"Hey, Uncle Raddix, Dominic, look, he's doing it again." Dean pointed at what Damon hoped wasn't too silly of a face.

Raddix slapped him on the shoulder, jolting him from his creepy staring fit.

"Let's go." Raddix nudged his head toward the woman Damon couldn't take his eyes off.

"You think she's pretty, don't you, Daddy?" Darlene whispered in her dad's ear.

"I do, honey, but looks only get you so far. Your mom was pretty, too."

"Only on the outside. Harlyn must eat her makeup because she's gorgeous on the inside, too.

Damon laughed, and his soul took flight. He realized he'd taught his daughter, and hopefully his boys, too, that beauty on the inside was more important than the outside.

Chapter 24

The entire town had shown up for the Man Hunt game, minus Selena, who would hopefully never step on ranch's soil again. She hadn't met the woman directly, but she'd heard enough about her that Harlyn wanted to stay clear of that trouble. Harlyn wanted to be in the sheriff's group—he must be good at hunting people, right?

No such luck.

Harlyn had never played this for fun before. The last decade, she had been the victim of a real-life Manhunt game. The best she could compare it to was hide n' seek in reverse. Since it was a large group playing, they broke into smaller teams for hiding purposes. The goal was to hunt down and tag the team of people hiding before they could reach ghouls, which was the post next to the horse corral.

It was nice to play at night's end so Cash and Carolyn could play, too. They were on a team with Amelia, Quinton, and Emmanuel. She found their taunting and goading entertaining, wildly when Raddix fired back with promises of finding them.

Harlyn didn't believe they'd get through more than one round. The ranch seemed to go on forever, but what did she know? She spied Raddix and Damon whispering to one another, probably creating an infallible plan to win.

As Quinton announced the rest of the teams, Harlyn moved beside Damon.

"Hey." He gave her an unexpected smile.

"Hey, yourself, Cowboy." She bumped his shoulder, but like a statue, he didn't move. Heat radiated off his body. "You're warm, she moved even closer."

"I see you're going to steal my body heat now, too?"

She smiled and nodded, knowing he was referring to losing his bed. His large arm wrapped around her shoulders. He turned her toward his side. Instinctively, she wrapped her arms around his middle.

"Is that okay?" His deep voice sent shivers down her spine. She nodded once again. To his credit, he respected the no-touching rule by asking if it was okay. He was sweet. Knowing he didn't want to be *sweet*, Harlyn wouldn't tell him that.

"You can have your bed back once you tell me whatever is so complicated for you."

Harlyn was partnered with Raddix, Lily, Damon, and Darlene. Their team would hide first. Those doing the hunting went inside the main house, giving the five hiders a chance to collaborate.

Raddix took Darlene's hand, "Come with us." They took off running.

Damon grabbed Harlyn's hand. "You, come with me."

She tried to ignore the tingling swirls navigating through her fingers as Damon laced his with hers and pulled her along.

Joy bubbled inside her as she raced across the ranch with her husband.

They were running down a newly made path when they heard a bullhorn, indicating the hunters were on the prowl.

"Quick, let's go."

"Okay, Daddy Longlegs," Harlyn joked. "One of your strides is like three of mine."

He stopped mid-stride, threw her over his shoulder like a sack of potatoes, and started running again.

"Damon," Harlyn barked out his name in a loud whisper, "Put me down. I wasn't that slow."

"Shh, you're going to get us caught."

They finally reached their hiding spot. "We're hiding in Raddix and Lily's house?"

"No, that would be against the rules," Damon grinned. "But, we are hiding in here."

Damon lifted the lid to a newly constructed storage box. This must have been what Damon and Raddix were whispering about. Fortunately, Darlene wasn't with them. Harlyn wasn't sure this was a good idea.

"How do you expect both of us to fit in here?" I'll get in and lay down, then you'll slide in after I get situated."

Damon rushed in and laid flat on his back.

"I'm not laying on top of you," Harlyn exclaimed, her heartbeat picking up. She was finally getting some sleep with Damon on the couch. She could not keep her wits about her in this situation.

"Come on, I don't want to get caught."

"Not my problem."

"I'm detecting that someone is still mad, or maybe the problem is you're too attracted to me, and you're afraid you might not be able to control yourself in here."

His playful grin was irritating. How could he be so right and so wrong at the same time? Harlyn had more self-control in her little pinky than most people had in their entire bodies. At least, she used to. She wouldn't have survived childhood if she hadn't.

Rustling in the woods startled Harlyn.

"Quick, get in."

She hoisted herself over the side, but Damon took up the entire space, so she landed on him.

"Umph!"

"Sorry." Harlyn pulled the cover down, leaving them in the pitch black.

Damon tugged her close to his chest. "Relax." He pulled her down, resting her head in the crook between his chest and shoulder. He placed his hand on her head, weaving his fingers through her hair. She hoped no one found them for a long while.

After a few moments of silence, he asked, "Could we talk?"

"If you're ready to tell me whatever is going on with you, I'd love to." Absently mindedly, she drew circles on his chest with her free hand, appreciating the results of his hard, laboring work. Nothing had ever energized her more. Her other arm, squished between them, would be numb in no time, but she couldn't care less.

His heart thundered in her ear, catching Harlyn off guard. He was too fit for that short run to cause his heart to beat that much out of control. Did she elicit that feeling in him?

"I'll do anything to get back into *my* bed," Damon joked, squeezing her shoulder, jolts of electricity ricocheting throughout her body.

She pushed out a quick, frustrated breath. Would he say anything just to avoid sleeping on the couch? On the other hand, she wanted to know everything going on with him. Harlyn wanted to be his support system like a real husband and wife.

How was she supposed to have a conversation crammed in a box draped over a man well over six foot, broad-shouldered, and this close? She could smell the faint spiciness of the cologne she discerned that morning, hay, and leather. Add that to them touching each other—a fog washed over her brain.

"Shouldn't we keep moving?" Harlyn managed to ask, hopefully not sounding too breathless.

"Are you trying to avoid the conversation?"

"Not at all. I want to win." Harlyn was competitive.

"Before we go, will you listen to me?"

"Go ahead."

"I'd wanted to spend time with Tanner, not knowing when I'd see him again once he leaves for the NRF. I'm sorry if I upset you."

"Is that all?" His silence revealed his answer. He hesitated another couple of seconds. "Brockton sent goons to rough me up."

She gasped.

"See," he gently lay her head back on his chest. "That's why I didn't say anything." He ran his fingers down her shoulder. "I can't stand seeing you upset."

"I need to leave. You, the kids, and all the people on this ranch are in danger. I can't bring that to my friends."

"You're not leaving. We're all safe here."

"I don't know about that."

"Let's move," Damon suggested as Harlyn slowly lifted the lid, peeking out into the day's dusk. Beautiful swirls of purple and pink filled the sky.

Running through the back, wooded area, Harlyn asked, "Can we get to my motorhome from here?"

"Great idea." He grabbed her hand, pulling her along. They were light on their feet, trying to avoid snapping twigs or crunching the fallen dead leaves.

Her stomach tightened when she spotted part of a white dress shirt with a small B imprinted on the pocket hanging from a branch.

"Brockton's been here." Panic spread through Harlyn. He was a lunatic following her around. *Find another woman already!* Her mind screamed. What could he possibly want? He came from money, so that couldn't be the motive.

"Leave it. We'll tell Gerard when the game is over."

He tugged on her arm gently, but her mortar-clad feet secured her position.

Harlyn eyed him cautiously. What if his good deed, trying to protect her, got him hurt? His kids needed him.

"Come on. We need to move." His authoritative, yet soothing command captured Harlyn's attention and freed her feet.

Once they reached her motorhome, they were surprised to find Raddix, Lily, and Darlene. Seeing the little girl's face set off alarms ringing in Harlyn's head. "What's wrong?"

"I'm sorry. We broke this." Darlene held up a cupboard door. "Raddix was trying to hide me in your cupboard above your couch. I got scared and kicked." Her soft voice, filled with regret, pulled at Harlyn's heart.

"Are you okay?" Harlyn balanced on the balls of her feet, getting eye level with the little girl who nodded her head. "Then that's all that matters."

"But that's nice," Darlene countered, pointing at the motorhome.

Before Harlyn could respond, Raddix pushed himself into the conversation. "I found some other interesting things."

Harlyn's expression bloomed with the prospect of finally having her freedom. Her eyes widened, and hope sparked in her chest. "Show me, please."

Damon startled at her excitement, causing a twinge of guilt to etch her stomach. She knew she should have told him everything about her past by now but hadn't.

Chapter 25

Damon's nerves returned like a boomerang when the concern embossed on Harlyn's face revealed more to her past than she'd led on.

Tagging along behind Harlyn, he hoped whatever Raddix found wouldn't pull Harlyn away from him. If it did, it would be his own fault for not telling her sooner. He had real feelings for her—more than the desire to protect her. Damon wanted them to be real husband and wife in every way.

His mind raced with ideas for dates. She'd love anything that involved her taking pictures, and Big Sky Country wouldn't disappoint. She'd mentioned going to Glacier National Park. Damon wanted to be beside her to watch her sunshiny persona light up.

He'd kept quiet about his feelings because he cared. The loving way she cared for the kids, her smile, and their teasing banter made it impossible for him to walk away. The last thing he wanted was to add to her stress about her past or make her nervous around him so he'd let her make the decisions regarding their relationship. Harlyn had let her no-touching rule slide a little, but he hadn't taken that as anything except her growing comfortable with him. That was very different from the feelings he had for her.

Hopefully, she'll understand that I didn't tell her so that I could protect her. He shook his head. Nothing ever went that easy. He knew if she kept something big from him, he'd be hurt; if that happened, his anger would get the best of him.

Chapter 26

A long, hollowed-out section at the top of her motorhome revealed a hidden door.

"Did you know this existed?" Damon rubbed her shoulder, stabilizing her nerves.

"No." Harlyn gripped her hair and dropped it onto the front of her shoulder. She began rubbing the clasp on her necklace.

"Here, let me." She felt Damon's warm breath all the way to her toes. Then, his fingers lightly brushed against the skin on the back of her neck. A cool, tingling sensation on her quads stole her attention.

"Thank you." She stared at the key in her hand. Feeling his gaze on her, Harlyn met Damon's eyes. The intensity beneath his dark eyes reeled her in, and she closed the gap between them. "I'm scared," she whispered.

He pulled her into his arms. "C'mon. You're the toughest person I know."

She pushed out a breath. "You must not know as many people as I thought you did."

He laughed and kissed the top of her head. "I'll spot you. Ready?"

A far-off coyote howl produced goosebumps on her arms. Fear. If she wasn't careful, danger lingered in these woods, especially with Brockton near. A coyote's motives were clear—it needed to eat. Brockton's sinister motives were unclear to her, making this situation even worse.

"Yup." He cupped her elbow, assisting her onto the table. When her eyes spotted the keyhole, her stomach flipped. Had she finally found it? Thick anticipation sucked all the air out of her motorhome. The key slid in easily. She let out an exaggerated breath, praying silently that her key opened the door and she got answers. A quick twist of the key and her heart leaped as she opened the door.

Reaching in, she pulled out a rolled piece of parchment, reminding her of the Declaration of Independence. Her mouth dropped as she rolled out the paper, revealing a map of an island off the coast of Greece, resting on the Mediterranean. The title at the top read 'Summers Family Estate, 1867', and a miniature blueprint of a castle was directly below the map.

"Will you take this, please?" She handed Damon the rolled map and grabbed an envelope from the secret compartment. Her eyes bugged out, and her jaw slackened.

"What's wrong?" Damon squeezed her waist and pulled her to the floor.

Tears pooled in her eyes. "This is what Grandpa was talking about," she said, handing him the paperwork revealing an offshore account in her name. "Ten years ago, the day before Grandpa died, marked the last deposit."

Damon's skeptical eyes stared at her. "Is your family rich? Who has eighty-three million dollars in this format? I could see being *worth* that much, but this is cash!" His voice rose, making Harlyn nervous. Hopefully, he'd understand when she told him the whole story about how much she already had secured in different accounts. She had to speak with Stan and Richard, too, but first, she'd explain everything to her husband.

"My grandpa told me to accept his will at face value. It left my mother one million dollars. Before I left, he'd opened an account for me with seventy million dollars." Collectively, jaws dropped, and the adults sent Darlene off to play.

"Aw, we want to hear this, too," she protested.

"It'll make for a good bedtime story some night, Sweetie." Harlyn hugged her and sent her on her way.

Damon whispered, "You're a millionaire. Why didn't you tell me?"

"Something like that," she responded vaguely. "I didn't know anything about this, so I'm just as shocked as you. I'm sorry. I should have told you my hold story by now, but you got so upset when I told you a little; I didn't want to really blow our mind."

Damon cleared his throat, almost like a cue for Raddix and Lily to explore the motorhome and hopefully find Darlene before they all got caught. A glance at Harlyn's watch revealed only five more minutes in the game. If no one found them, they won.

Harlyn stared at Damon as he invaded her space. His warm arms, like vice grips around her waist, felt comforting. "I will always get angry when people hurt you." He leaned even closer. "Now that you are my wife, I won't let anyone hurt you ever again."

His comments struck her like bolts of lightning right in the heart. *Aw. That's so sweet.*

Suddenly, the door flew open, and the seekers found them with two minutes to spare.

Harlyn and Damon brought the Sheriff to the spot in the woods, revealing Brockton had trespassed. "This is a new tactic for Brockton, I think," Harlyn shared.

"How so?" Sheriff McDugal dropped the white shirt into the evidence bag Deputy Williams brought him.

Harlyn wrapped her arms around her middle. "He'd show up once every couple of years in public places and then be gone. If my bodyguards saw him more, they never told me."

"When did you get rid of your guards?" Gerard asked.

"Right before I came here. Brockton got close enough to grab me a couple of years ago, but Jet, my lead security at the time, took care of him. When we didn't see Brockton again, and I had the interview for this job, I let them go. Most of them had been with me since I was nineteen, and I didn't want them to relocate their families again. They were paid well and deserved to enjoy their time with their loved ones.

"I bet they were paid very well." Damon's voice lacked the cadence with which she'd become familiar.

It wasn't her fault she had all this money. Maybe she should have told Damon everything earlier, but she hadn't wanted to see the angered expression that currently masked his face.

"Are we okay to leave, Sheriff? My wife and I have a lot to discuss."

She swallowed . . . hard. Maybe they *had* reached the *share everything* moment in their relationship.

"Sure. Please text me day or night if you think of anything else."

"Thank you."

Harlyn looked around. Everyone had left them except for Quinton, Amelia, and Gerard. As Damon said farewell to everyone, Gerard said, "Don't get too grumpy with her. She's already been through enough." The others echoed his sentiments.

He was about to find out the ugly truth of what he'd married into. *Lord, I am so scared right now. Damon will find out all the dirtiness of my childhood and leave me. I'll be alone again.*

Chapter 27

Damon stocked out of the motorhome right past her without much of a glance. She ran to catch him but had to hop-skip now and then to keep up with him and his long stride. He should have slowed down but didn't.

"Where are you headed?" Harlyn placed her hand on his forearm, and he jerked it away. She stopped.

"Whatever. Be mad. When you're ready to be a big boy and talk, I'll be in the greenhouse."

That stopped him. He turned, half expecting Harlyn to stare at him, waiting for him to give in and talk, but she wasn't. She'd already turned around, presumably headed toward the greenhouse like she said.

If I'm the mad one... he couldn't even complete a single thought. *What the heck is going on here?*

The tightness in his chest and shoulders coiled up more. Cheryl also left Damon to himself when he got mad. Don't women understand men have feelings, too? *She was chasing after you. How'd you expect her to stop you?*

"Shut up," he scolded himself aloud.

With a huff, he dragged his feet toward the greenhouse. *You know, you're no better than her. You'd just been thinking about keeping secrets from her to protect her; maybe you should listen to her before you condemn her.*

"Touché, God. Thanks for the reminder." Damon said aloud, truly appreciating the Holy Spirit living within him,

When he reached the greenhouse door, he inhaled dramatically and let it out.

Upon opening the door, he didn't see Harlyn. Then, a blast of cold water hit his chest. "What are you doing?"

Damon jumped, placing his forearms in front of his face to block as much water as possible.

"Watering the plants. Sorry, the hose slipped," she said, removing her finger from the trigger. The heavy water spraying her husband ceased, and he relaxed his arms.

He bit his lip to prevent himself from laughing. This woman brought out the best in him.

"I'm sorry for the way I acted." He inched closer to Harlyn, who was still holding the sprayer like a water gun ready to blast. The pressure felt like a fire hose, so he hoped to appease her before she pulled the trigger again.

"Mm-hmm." She tightened her grip on the metal handle. "You wouldn't even listen to me. I'm sorry I didn't tell you about my past. Do you have any idea what my life has been like? Unable to trust anyone, I keep my thoughts and feelings to myself."

He stepped even closer. "Will you please put that down? It's not summer anymore." She dropped the mechanism on its handle, and it sprayed out on his boots.

"I'm sorry." She kicked it with her foot, stopping the water.

Damon stuffed his hands in his pockets. His boots were inches from hers. "Let me talk first, okay?" She nodded. "I was hurt, and anger is how I express myself when that happens." He reached for her hands and laced his fingers with hers. "I realized I wasn't any better than you because I've been keeping something from you, too, and it's not fair for me to be a hypocrite."

Her brows lifted, probably wondering what he was keeping from her. He'd been rambling. Sweat formed under his hat and arms. If he put himself out there again, Harlyn could break his heart, and there'd be no coming back from it. His feelings for her were already stronger than they had been for Cheryl. It took him meeting Harlyn to realize that he and Cheryl were not suitable for each other and had no business ever pretending to love each other. That didn't mean he would change anything, though. His time with Cheryl gave him Dean, Dominic, and Darlene—his favorite people in the world.

"I don't want to be your fake husband anymore." The tightening of his chest returned but for a different reason. His sternum, ribs, and lungs were constricted, protecting his vulnerable heart.

Her tongue poked out between her lips, and a glaze formed over her eyes. "I get it. No hard feelings. Dealing with Brockton and my parents—"

"—I want to be husband and wife for real," he interrupted, shaking their linked hands slightly, jolting her.

She shook her head. "I can't handle that right now. I have to talk to Stan and Richard. There's so much I have to tell you. I don't even know what all the maps and accounts mean. My grandpa told me. . ."

"You can trust me," Damon tried to reassure her.

Harlyn released their hands, stepping back. She turned, wrapping her arms around her middle. Damon layered his arms on top of hers, pressing her back onto his chest. "Don't be scared. I'll wait until you're comfortable. Make your calls, do whatever you need, but promise me one thing . . . you won't run. I can protect you here, and I will."

"I promise."

Chapter 28

Over the next few days, Harlyn noticed less red on the thermometer, which was grating her nerves. Central Montana was the polar opposite of Arizona.

Not that she wanted to go back there. Heck no. Wherever Damon and the kids were was where she wanted to be.

So much so that she agreed not to run off even though she knew Brockton was on his way with reinforcement—hopefully not the same goons from the dance hall. Yeah, Damon had finally told her about the fight.

He'd also told Harlyn that he wanted to be her real husband. She'd dreamed of that since. Neither Stan nor Richard had returned her call. She wouldn't endanger Damon any more than she already had until she knew how the castle and money impacted Damon and his kids.

After saying goodnight to the kids, she leaned over the island counter. Harlyn let out an audible "Mmmm" as her black raspberry ice cream coated her mouth and throat.

Damon's shoulder brushed up against hers. "Wanna share?" His impish grin was nearly irresistible.

"Nope." Harlyn popped the 'p' before she turned the spoon upside down on her tongue. She let the ice cream fall into her mouth, then slowly pulled the spoon out.

Damon's eyes were glued to each movement she made, prompting Harlyn to repeat her actions. The idea of sharing her ice cream with him seemed so intimate. Harlyn prayed for a husband like Damon. One she'd laugh with, be mesmerized entirely by, and one who'd protect and love her. Three out of four wasn't bad. There was no way he could love her.

He bumped her shoulder, forcing her back into the moment. Her spoon hung inches away from her mouth. "Thank you for dinner; it was great."

"You're welcome." His praise and appreciation warmed her deep within.

He draped his arm over her shoulder, sliding even closer to her side. "Could I please have a little dessert?" his warm breath settled on her cheek.

"Excuse me?"

He nodded toward the ice cream. Her cheeks heated and were probably scarlet if the heat she felt was any indication. The idea of her being dessert. Wow. That was a very husbandly thing to say. But he wasn't her real husband, so she needed to think of something else. With him so close, it was nearly impossible.

"What were you thinking?" his chuckle did funny things to her insides.

She opened her mouth to say something but quickly shoved the ice cream spoon inside, ignoring this question.

Harlyn scraped the sides of the pint, filling her spoon with more ice cream. But this time, she pointed it in Damon's direction. He closed his eyes and opened his mouth, allowing Harlyn to feed him the milky dessert.

"Mmm. That's good." He opened his eyes, connecting with hers. The longing there told her this marriage might be everything she had always wanted.

"Harlyn." Hearing her name in his low, gravelly voice stole her breath away. "I think there's more. . ." She swallowed a lump the size of Texas, waiting for him to finish.

Damon took the spoon from her hand and jammed it into the ice cream in the carton, puncturing the soft, cardboard bottom. He cupped her cheek. "There could be more between us. I won't pressure you to be my real wife, but I want to kiss you right now."

Her eyes dropped to his lips as he slowly moistened them with his tongue. Kiss? Unless his gaze stole her hearing, too, Damon just admitted he wanted things to get physical.

"I'm not stopping you." She tilted her head, studying his handsome face. *Where did that come from?*

His knuckles caressed her cheek as he leaned in. He wrapped his other hand around her waist, turning her toward him.

Her heart raced almost as fast as the pulse on his neck. She reached up, grazing her fingers over the spot. When he visibly shivered, she smiled, knowing the effect she had on him. At that moment, she realized she'd give up the castle, the island, every penny in her name, so it didn't matter what Stan or Richard had to say. *Lord, if I'm being reckless, acting on my feelings, please stop me. Please keep Damon, his kids, and everyone on the ranch safe.* "Once you kiss me, there will be no turning back," Harlyn breathed.

"That's good because I already told you what I want." The combination of Damon's husky voice and the thirstiness in his eyes sent her into a series of flips and jumps like Simone Biles's Olympic Trials floor routine.

Hope bloomed inside her, and sparks of electricity filled the air. She would finally share her feelings with him. Harlyn could swear his breath hitched. His firm lips grazed over hers for a nanosecond. *That definitely wasn't even a real kiss.*

"Dad!" Darlene screamed, pulling them apart. His conflicted eyes pained her. Did he feel like he had to choose? This wasn't a contest.

"Go make sure she's okay. I'll clean up," Harlyn whispered. Their moment, lost.

Um, Lord, was that just happenstance or a sign?

The following morning, she opened the bathroom door and found him shirtless, holding onto the top molding. His biceps popped even more when he leaned in and asked, "Can my wife share the bathroom? Meadow is waiting for me."

"Meadow, huh?" On their own accord, Harlyn's eyes roam over him appreciatively. "You're lucky I know Meadow is a horse, or you'd be on the couch again."

His belly laugh filled the room, causing a burst of happiness inside Harlyn.

"Jealous much?"

"Not even in your wildest dreams, Cowboy," she chuckled. It's not like she'd memorized every ridge in his arms. Only the few that settled nicely at her eye level. What else was she supposed to look at?

The carry-over tension between them from the night before was electrifying, making Harlyn want his kiss even more.

He blocked her exit with his arm. His lips grazed right below her earlobe, and in the huskiest voice she'd ever heard, he said, "There's no reason for you to be jealous. I'm all yours."

What!? She sucked in a breath; he wasn't allowed to say things like that when her resistance was low. A whirlpool of desire blasted into her belly, and heat rose in her neck. She had to fan herself.

"Harlyn!" Darlene hollered from her room. "Will you come here, please?"

"Saved by the child." She ducked under Damon's arm and hurried out the bedroom door.

When she heard him let out a sigh, Harlyn looked over her shoulder and found him peering around the door frame, watching her escape.

When the kids raced to the main house for school, Damon shared his schedule for the day—it was packed—training Meadow with Tanner and working with a new stang he was trying to break in the morning. Then, his Hippotherapy group and his neurodivergent group filled his afternoon. Right before he ate dinner, he'd get the horses ready to relax for the evening. She was tired just hearing what he would be doing all day.

By lunchtime, Harlyn was done with her chores. The greenhouse plants had already sprouted. The regular customers would buy their starter plants at the ranch in a few months. Pride filled Harlyn every day she saw the reward of her hard work.

"Harlyn, over here," Lily hollered from the porch on the main house where she gathered with Amelia, Reneé, and Carolyn.

As she hustled toward them, she spied the men at their usual table (fifty feet from the women). This reminded her of high school, where all the popular guys sat at one table, and the girls sat at theirs. *I'm married to one of the popular guys!* Her inner thoughts squealed.

The kids played on the swing set and climbing equipment while Reneé took a well-deserved break. Harlyn had helped out in the classroom, and man, she wondered how that woman was upright at dinner time.

Darlene rushed off the swings and wrapped her arms around Harlyn's waist. "Can you swing with me?"

"How about you swing with your friends now, and once school is out, we'll do something together?"

"Okay. Thank you, Harlyn." Darlene ran off to swing with Emmanuel.

"You've made a friend for life," Amelia proclaimed as Harlyn climbed the porch steps.

It scared Harlyn how much she'd grown to love Damon's kids. Unlike what her parents had shown her, she'd always wanted to be a mother so she could give kids the love they deserve.

Harlyn recalled when she was young, her dad played Barbies with her. Then, once she started Kindergarten, her dad turned evil like her mother. The pain from his neglect still stung today. That's why she always made herself available whenever Darlene asked anything of her.

Dominic and Dean rarely pressed Harlyn. They were too busy wrestling with their dad or playing ball. She'd be there whenever they did need her.

"Ladies, we have a victim here," Lily crooned, causing the women to burst into a peal of laughter, gaining the men's attention.

Harlyn's eyes instantly found Damon's. While he looked divine in his blue flannel shirt, unbuttoned at the top and his sleeves rolled up to his elbows, exposing the coil ridges in his forearms, all Harlyn could think of were his rock-hard, bare chest and abs that branded her brain earlier that morning.

"You know you're the best thing that has ever happened to him, right?" Amelia stated with a gentle voice.

Harlyn stole another glimpse at Damon and scoffed. "No, I believe Dean, Dominic, and Darlene were."

She couldn't stop stewing about Brockton. How did he keep finding her? Harlyn refused to let that pompous jerk hurt Damon or his kids.

As a teenager, Harlyn often chose to spend time with Brockton's parents over him when Nancy forced Harlyn to visit. By then, everything with him had been about money and power, but his parents had still been relatable. Apparently, her parents had corrupted him.

He knew most of the Summers's money was Nancy's. Old money from her family that got handed down from generation to generation. A memory of Nancy's harsh words came rushing back. "Harlyn, you're not worth a dime of my money. You best find yourself a rich man because you're not getting any of this."

Seriously? Harlyn didn't care about money. That was the truth even before her mother's dad gifted her more money than she or the next six generations of heirs could possibly spend. That was also after she'd donated millions to worthy causes.

After meeting Emmanuel, Harlyn anonymously donated millions to two organizations she overheard Quinton talking about. These organizations were instrumental in getting him and his late wife the resources they needed for Emmanuel when he was younger.

"You know," Reneé's soft voice broke into Harlyn's thoughts. "I've noticed a difference in Damon since Rocco, the kids, and I have returned." The other women nodded in agreement.

"How so?" Harlyn focused her attention on Reneé

"He's not as grumpy."

The ladies stared off at the men's table where they were engaged in a lively conversation with pushing and shoving.

"Men are strange creatures," Lily giggled. "They always have to be touching something. It's in their DNA."

Amelia's face brightened. "Thank God for that."

The women gasped, and Reneé's shriek, "Amelia!" reached the men. They stopped instantly, staring at the ladies, who waved their fingers in their direction.

"That's one of the perks of being married. It makes up for all the trouble they cause otherwise." More fits of laughter clearly intrigued the men because they sauntered over.

"What trouble are you ladies causing over here?" Raddix eyed his wife with smoldering eyes that set Harlyn's heart soaring, hoping to get the same look from Damon.

"No trouble." Lily shrugged, feigning an innocent look.

"Doubtful since you are now in cahoots with The Troublesome Trio."

"Don't exclude my wife," Quinton spoke up.

"Mine either," Rocco smiled at Reneé.

Tanner slapped Damon on the shoulder, probably wanting him to say something about the Mrs., but he remained silent.

He is the best fake husband. . . ever!

Chapter 29

"The night air in late October is colder here than I remember it being in Connecticut." She shivered, making Damon wish he had a jacket for her. They'd been roaming around the ranch, talking like teenagers about their pasts.

He began unbuttoning his heavy chamois, but her slender fingers covered his, stopping him. "You're not giving me that. You probably only have a t-shirt under there." She wasn't wrong, but he'd weather the cold for her.

"What good is having a fake husband if he can't warm you up?" He tenderly removed her hand, kissed her knuckles, and removed his shirt. After placing it around her shoulders, he rubbed his palms up and down her arms.

Damon would endure anything for Harlyn, so it hurt so much when he learned about her entire past. In a no-holds-barred style, she told Damon how she'd grown up, which explained why she was so strong. After living like she had, a person could go one of two ways: retreat into a shell and be taken advantage of or be stronger than ever. That was Harlyn.

Most women needed a man for something, be it financial, emotional, or spiritual. Not Harlyn. She didn't need Damon for anything. Technically, she didn't even need the fake marriage. She could live in her motorhome with bodyguards for the rest of her life. Money was a joke—she had more than he could even comprehend. Her faith was probably stronger than his, too. All around, she was tougher than a bull protecting his cow.

The news of her past had been a blow to Damon. He wondered if he should have been smarter and guarded his heart better. He'd laid his feelings out for her—he wanted to be her *real* husband. Since she hadn't brought that topic up again, he dropped it, not wanting to make her uncomfortable.

A bone-crushing feeling came over him—when it was safe, Harlyn would probably leave. What would he tell the kids? His heart? All of them loved Harlyn.

"What's wrong, Damon?" Harlyn brushed his forearm.

Tell her.

She waited.

Nope. Not yet. "Tell me about your grandparents."

"I love them. One time, my grandmother traipsed out in the backyard during Nancy's book club, wearing nothing but a bikini. She said, 'If your mother is going to call me crazy, I'll show her what crazy looks like.'"

They laughed. Harlyn stumbled on the uneven ground. Grabbing Damon's arm, she righted herself. "Sorry." She smiled, warming him all over.

"Your arm is freezing. Take this back." She pulled his shirt off her shoulders and shoved it in his unaccepting hands.

"You're stubborn," he grumbled.

"Are you to the pot or the kettle?" Her sassy comeback flickered flames in his low belly.

"Which one do you want me to be?"

Her frozen expression was precisely what he'd hoped for. The words weren't romantic, but his tone was certainly suggestive and hit his mark. Before the silence became any more awkward, he returned to their topic of discussion. "What was your mother referring to when she spoke of a deal about you marrying Brockton?"

"I wish I knew. Brockton's parents are wealthy. His dad groomed him for the family business, so I can't imagine any deals he would need."

"Something doesn't make sense," Damon challenged. "If they have money and power, why don't they find someone else for him to marry?"

"You'd think they would. My Grandpa told me years ago that it has something to do with the map."

"If your mother expected to inherit your Grandpa's wealth and apparently a castle, I'm afraid she won't rest until she gets it."

"Maybe." Harlyn brushed up against his shoulder, setting off sparkling sensations all the way to his fingers. "My gut tells me there's more to this."

"Whatever it is, I'll be here for you until you toss me aside."

Harlyn tugged his arm, forcing him to stop. "I'm not Cheryl," her tone was harsh but then softened. "I will never be able to repay you for your unselfish act. Marrying me to keep me safe means more than all the money, castles, and whatever else is all tied up in this mess." Harlyn leaned in, kissing his smooth cheek, branding him forever with her.

"The pleasure has been all mine. Even couch surfing is worth it if you're happy."

The intensity in her eyes peeked at a different level than he was used to. She still hadn't removed her hand from his arm. He squared his shoulders in front of her and searched her face, trying to find his own strength to continue.

"You are eons away from being my ex-wife. You're selfless, kind, hard-working, and beautiful when you don't even try. I let Cheryl take a lot from me, unintentionally, of course. She would never visit my parents or let them come here. Once Cheryl started taking her own little vacations, I flew my parents to me. I should have seen it then, but the idea of having a wife blinded me. It wasn't until the last time I saw my parents that my mom finally told me she couldn't stand Cheryl—said she was controlling and manipulative— 'not worthy of my son' were her exact words."

"Smart woman." They shared an intimate smile.

"My dad didn't like to cause waves, whereas mom was the earthquake that spurred the tsunami."

"Sounds like my kind of woman," Harlyn let out a cheerful laugh.

Damon pulled Harlyn flush with his chest. "You two would have most likely had words at some point, knowing both of you, but you would have loved each other, too."

"Damon." He loved the sound of his name on her lips. "I know it hurts that they're gone, but honor them the best way you can—be happy."

You make me happy. They still hadn't revisited the idea of this marriage being real, but he'd do everything he could to show her it was real.

"Will you go to the fall dance with me?" Damon pleaded silently. *Please make her say yes.*

"It would be an honor."

"The honor is all my, Sweetheart." Harlyn had trespassed on his heart, but now she was a welcomed, hopefully permanent, resident.

Chapter 30

Lightning danced across the night sky. Everyone on the ranch said this weather was unheard of at the end of October. "Don't be surprised if we have snow next week," Jeff stated matter-of-factly.

Quinton stuck to Amelia as he guided her across the parking lot toward the dance hall entrance. Raddix and Lily ushered Emmanuel closely behind.

Harlyn sympathized with Amelia's struggle with storms. Harlyn had weathered storms all her life, but Amelia had difficulty with literal storms since her aunt, Raddix's mom, died in a storm. Just recently, news of Raddix's dad, Sean, saving his son in that storm but unable to save his wife explained why Sean had isolated himself for so long.

The entire ranch family embraced him a few nights ago. In an attempt to heal, Sean had been working with his Daughter-In-Law, Lily, to deal with his emotions.

"I'm sure Violet would be there to support you as well, Dad, if you let her."

"One step at a time, Son."

When Quinton opened the door, loud music jolted Harlyn back to the present. Kids and parents from neighboring towns danced, played games in one corner, ate, and drank in another. Fall-colored streamers looped from one beam to the next. Some kids dressed up, but most didn't. Instead, they engaged in fun activities, building memories with friends and family.

"This looks so fun." Watching the kids laugh and play pierced Harlyn's heart, reminding her that she lost her childhood at the hands of her sadistic parents. They were interfering with her adult life, too. She felt the tears in her eyes but refused to let them surface.

"Are you okay, Sweetheart?"

"I like seeing kids having fun. I never got to do that," Harlyn whispered, placing her hand on his bicep.

Holy Moly! Did he just flex? His muscles weren't new to her. They'd tortured her every night and every morning before Damon covered them with his shirt, but they felt different. Or maybe she felt different about Damon, making him even more appealing.

His strong arms wrapped around her waist. She shivered at the jolt of electricity that shot through her body.

"Would you like to dance?"

His milk chocolate eyes reached hers. Their intensity made her heart flutter. When his gaze dropped to her lips, her pulse quickened. He hated to dance, but he asked her to anyway. *He's so sweet. Why me, Lord? He could have any woman he wanted, yet he chose to marry me so I'd be safe.* Harlyn's heart beat wildly against her rib cage.

"Harlyn." The way her name rolled off his tongue, low and endearing, clogged her thinking.

"Could you allow blood to flow through my arm again, or do you plan on taking it as a souvenir?"

Red-hot embarrassment sped up her neck and settled in her cheeks. She resisted the urge to fan herself, not wanting to draw even more attention to herself.

"Sorry," she huffed out, releasing his arm.

Darlene appeared at their sides, naturally creating space between them. "Dad, we're taking Emmanuel to the games to meet the other kids."

She looked at Emmanuel's little hands fiddling with each other. Her heart melted watching him shift side to side. The sheer panic written all over his face starkly contrasted his time on the ranch with people he was comfortable around.

"Be patient with him. Damon lifted his eyes. Emmanuel tugged his cowboy hat below his eyes, and his rocking side to side picked up speed.

Darlene motioned for her dad to lean down but spoke loud enough for Harlyn to hear. "I'll watch out for him. If anyone says anything mean, I'll allow them to apologize like you said. If they don't, I'll make sure they never say another mean word about him again."

Damon had taught his kids how to stick up for themselves respectfully.

"Don't be too bold. You might embarrass Emmanuel. Give him the courage to stand up for himself."

"Good point, Dad, you boys have fragile egos."

Darlene skipped away, happy as ever. Harlyn slapped her hand over her mouth to cover her laughter.

Damon hid the smile she saw forming. "Not one word." His eyes fixated on her.

"Oh, of course not. I'd hate to see your fragile ego get bruised, too."

Damon tugged her by the waist, flush with his side. "You'll pay for that."

"I'm so scared," she feigned nervousness.

"Woohoo, Harlyn, over here." Hazel and Myrtle shuffled toward her while Lily trailed behind.

Damon fled, as he suggested, "Don't let them corrupt you, too."

Hazel peered at Harlyn through her oval glasses, giving her a more youthful appearance, but the wicked grin on her face revealed she was up to no good. In contrast, Myrtle's crow's feet and dark hair, peppered with gray, revealed her age—seventy-two, at least. The familiar floral scent permeated the air, announcing Doris's arrival, but Harlyn hadn't seen her yet.

"Look at those two handsome hunks over there," Hazel winked at Harlyn and Lily as she pointed at Damon and Raddix.

Then, the older woman moved between Harlyn and Lily and hooked her arms through each woman's arm, dragging them away and declaring, "We have work to do."

This was the most fun Harlyn had ever had. After getting directions from Hazel, Harlyn, and Lily filled their husbands in since the plan involved them.

"You take the first one," Raddix told Damon and Harlyn. "I'll never hear the end of it if you don't."

"I'm not keen on this idea," Damon declared, crossing his arms over his chest.

"We'll, it's happening, and unless you want me to interrupt Tanner over there," everyone turned to see him dancing with a girl, and they looked very cozy, "then you're stuck with me."

Damon's nostrils flared. "You're not dancing with Tanner."

His deep scowl and clenched jaw made his jealousy known. If that wasn't enough for Harlyn to feel wanted, Damon's eyes roamed over the length of her.

"Are you sure? I don't think he'd mind." She attempted to move toward Tanner, hoping Damon called her bluff.

Damon blocked her path, gripping her wrist tenderly. He leaned in, speaking into her hair. "Don't make me demote you to the couch. My wife will not dance with anyone but me."

Her stomach flip-flopped, watching the passion in his eyes grow more intense by the second. Harlyn wasn't even sure if Raddix and Lily were still with them. The loud music sounded muffled, like she was listening to it in a tunnel. All she saw was Damon—the man she'd lost her heart to—who vowed to keep her safe from Brockton.

"Your jealousy is kinda sexy," Harlyn admitted. She didn't want to upset him or bring up bad memories of all he'd been through with Cheryl. "You have nothing to worry about. There isn't another man alive I'd rather dance with." Her palms slowly rose over his chest and behind his neck.

"That's good because I'd hate to mess up Tanner right before his competition."

Her heart picked up speed as he leaned closer. Finally, they'd have their first kiss. Too bad there were so many people around, but at this point, she didn't care; they'd waited long enough.

Just as their lips were about to connect, a shrill from the speakers pulled them apart, forcing them to cover their ears. Instinctively, every adult from Big L' Ranch (that she could see) searched for Emmanuel. He had his hands on his ears and only screamed briefly until Quinton got to him, putting on his noise-canceling headphones. Darlene was right by his side, making sure he was okay with a thumbs up that he returned.

"She's good for him," Harlyn noted.

"Don't start. They are too young,"

Harlyn put her hands up in surrender. She wasn't encouraging ten-year-olds to date—no way, but Darlene was a great friend to Emmanuel.

Hazel tapped on the microphone, but people were ready for it this time. "We have the last song of the night, and it will be a little different.

"Gerard just looked at me. He knows something is up," Damon grumbled.

Harlyn rubbed this shoulder. "Don't worry, you are an accomplice; they go easier on them than the masterminds."

"You know this how?"

"True Crime podcast and TV shows," she shrugged, grinning ear to ear.

Damon opened his mouth to speak, but Hazel's voice radiated throughout the room. "Everyone will start dancing, almost like musical chairs. When the music stops, you find a new partner. Ready? Let the fun begin." Hazel winked at Harlyn.

Myrtle snagged Gerard before Hazel finished the instruction, and Harlyn nudged Damon to ask Willow to dance. Willow looked suspiciously at Harlyn.

"Now, I know the Troublesome Trio is up to something." She rested one hand on Damon's shoulder and the other in his waiting hand. "They won't lock Gerard and me in a closet again, will they?"

Harlyn giggled as she left the dance floor, leaving poor Damon to shrug his shoulders. She worked hard to read Damon's lips but couldn't. He was now leading Willow where he was supposed to, and Raddix was dancing with Violet. Finally, Lily had convinced her Father-in-Law to dance.

Less than a minute in, everyone was in a good position. Hazel stopped the music, and Damon twirled Willow right into Gerard's arms as Myrtle stepped out of the way. Raddix asked for his wife back and maneuvered Violet in his dad's direction.

"Damon, help me off the floor. My ankle's acting up," Myrtle ordered loud enough for everyone to hear. Given her age, it was plausible that she had an aliment, but she moved rather quickly toward Harlyn.

"Here's your hubby back, Dearie. Go enjoy the rest of the dance."

As they entered the dance floor together, Harlyn heard Sean speaking with Raddix. "We'll discuss this later, Son."

Harlyn mouthed, "Sorry." Raddix waved off her apology.

"Do you think that little stunt will make a difference?"

"I don't know," Harlyn began. "But the trio arranged our fake marriage, and that worked out okay, didn't it?"

"Better than okay." He caressed her back lazily as he closed the gap between them. "Have you thought any more about what I said?"

She knew what he meant, but that didn't mean she was ready to answer. "Richard called earlier. I told him to send hefty bonuses to every bodyguard who helped me over the years, and he donated significant amounts to my charity choices. The rest of the money has been transferred to accounts he set up here. I don't even know what to do with it."

"There's something you're not telling me. Please don't keep things from me."

He deserved the truth. "Richard said the island and castle can only be mine if I do not marry before I'm thirty, which, as you know, *husband*, isn't the case." She appreciated his attentiveness but wished he'd interrupt with questions to prolong the rest.

"Mm-hmm."

Harlyn let out a sigh. "Since we haven't consummated our marriage, we could get an annulment to resolve the issue."

"Is that what you want to do?"

It's more difficult than that, but he got the gist.

"I don't know."

Damon's arms went limp, and Harlyn's heart sank. He was pulling away from her.

Chapter 31

"Yes, I'm still here." Brockton ran his hand through his hair as he paced back and forth in front of the bed at the hotel where he'd been staying a couple of hours outside Haven Ridge.

"I want more than a picture this time."

Brockton couldn't imagine what else he had to do. The agreement had always been thirty grand for a picture and video of Harlyn's whereabouts with proof, such as a date and time stamp.

"Her bodyguards almost ripped me apart the last time I got close enough to touch her. Now she has a whole town protecting her."

He'd spent the last ten years following this woman around, watching her take pictures, gather with others at campsites, and jam out to the music she loved. Why did he have to continue enduring that pain? She wanted nothing to do with him since he stupidly sided with her enemies. Not that he'd been given a choice—he *had* to work for them.

"What else could you possibly want from me?"

A sinister chuckle on the other end of the line sent icy chills down Brockton's spine. "It's time to bring Harlyn home."

"How do you suppose I do that?"

He vowed never to get as close to her as he did at the Botanical Gardens in Arizona. In her little Mayberry town, with one sheriff and a deputy appearing more capable than Barney Fife, they wouldn't let him get anywhere near her.

"She has a husband protecting her. Our plan is shot. Can't we just find someone else for me to marry?"

"You fool! There is no one else!" Brockton was concerned by the panic in the woman's voice. She sounded desperate, and desperate people made rash decisions.

Brockton couldn't afford *not* to follow orders. His parents cut him off a decade ago when he didn't *seal the deal* and marry Harlyn. He realized too late that he was only a puppet for the powers that be—doing and saying whatever he was told or else. If her parents hadn't been so manipulative and controlling, causing Harlyn to run, there might have been a chance for the two of them. He longed for the simpler times when they were teens.

He remembered when he dressed up like a clown, making Harlyn laugh. She had the most pleasant laugh, making his heart swell. They could have been a power couple themselves if it hadn't been for their parents.

"I don't care how you get her here. Just do it!" Before Brockton could respond, the line disconnected.

He wanted to know how Harlyn had survived all these years without her parents' resources. Were they right? Had she stolen all her Grandpa's money? Her parents had already looked into the motorhome. Apparently Harold gifted it to her a few days before he died. Until the day Harold's attorney, Richard, read Mr. Summers's will, Brockton had never seen Harlyn's mom lose her temper, and he hoped he never saw it again. Most people would have been happy to receive a million dollars. Not her. She asked about castles and islands. That had been news to him. The attorney knew his job well. He repeated the same line multiple times without revealing any pertinent information that might lead them to Harlyn. "This is all that was in Harold's name at the time of his death."

Brockton recalled Nancy's beet-red face verbally sparring with the man.

"There are bylaws that need to be followed precisely for things to be legal," Nancy argued.

Richard never let the woman get to him. "Trust me, Harold knew what he was doing." He handed Nancy a check. "This is what you've been given. Nothing else is your concern."

Harlyn had always been honest, so everything he'd been told over the years since she'd been gone didn't seem legit. But none of that mattered now. He was in too deep and had a job to do. Brockton liked being rich. Each job kept the money coming in since his dad basically disowned him from their family business. He wouldn't hurt Harlyn, but she would be his ticket to wealth.

Now, how would he get her away from that hick cowboy?

Chapter 32

All Harlyn could think about was how she felt in Damon's arms, swaying to the music. Hazel never stopped it again once her couples were matched.

But then Harlyn had ruined the moment by opening her mouth. A chill ran up her spine when Damon released her and walked out the door. She didn't chase after him this time; that way, he couldn't do or say anything mean. Was he most upset about getting an annulment, or was it something else?

Harlyn had distracted herself, helping pick up. Doris finally revealed herself—she'd been hiding in the kitchen all night. Harlyn expected a story there, but the woman wasn't sharing anything. "Hazel's plan is working. Look at our two couples working together."

Sean and Gerard were setting up the tables that had been stored to make more room while Violet and Willow were stacking the chairs behind them.

"What makes you think those couples will stick?" Harlyn asked, thinking more about her and Damon.

"We just observe things that others don't or won't admit, and we put people in front of each other, not allowing them to chicken out. But that's not to say we're always right. We don't stop, though. People learn best from the mistakes they make."

Harlyn had heard Reneé tell the kids that every day. Maybe there was something to that idea.

She'd made a big mistake tonight by only telling Damon part of the situation. Hopefully, he'd listen to her once they got home. The surge of warmth that ran through her body thinking about having a home with Damon brought tears to her eyes. She blinked them back as the kids approached, ready to go home. Hopefully, she'd give Damon enough time to cool down.

After putting the kids to bed, Damon changed into sweatpants and a form-fitting shirt that stretched across his chest. Sitting on the couch, scrolling through channels, he didn't look her way when she sat beside him.

"Can we talk?"

Damon pressed the power button, dropped his feet to the floor, and placed the remote on the coffee table in front of him. He still hadn't said a word to her. It was a quiet ride home with Darlene sleeping and the boys listening to their music.

"Yeah." He rested his elbows on his knees and dropped his head into his palms.

That was progress. Harlyn didn't waste a second. "When I said that I didn't know, it had nothing to do with you or the feelings I've developed for you." Harlyn closed the gap between them and rubbed his shoulders. They were so close she could still smell his musky cologne. It was doing funny things to her stomach.

"Care to enlighten me?"

"If I give up the castle and island, the bylaws state that it has to go back to the closest living heir, which is my mother."

"So don't give it up," He finally looked at her.

"It's not that easy."

"Nothing ever is," Damon grumped.

"By accepting the property, I have to live there for at least a year before it can be used as a vacation spot for the rest of my life."

"That's not ideal, but if you want to be with me—"

There's more she cut him off with a gentle hand to his thigh, trying to comfort him after he plopped back against the couch, covering his face with his palms.

"My husband would have to live there with me because he would automatically be the King and take complete control over the castle and island."

His face paled instantly. He inched his body into a seated position. "You're kidding," she shook her head. "I can't be a King!" He shot to his feet, pacing the floor in front of the table. The quieter the room got, the more Harlyn's anxiety grew.

"Say something," she urged.

"Who's *the King* right now?"

"From what Richard said, they've been operating based on Grandpa's directives for the last ten years. The property comes with its own allotment of money. Richard has been using that to keep the army and all castle staff members employed. He's visited at least twice a year since my Grandpa died, and things are as smooth as they had been the last seventy years."

Her nervous heart sped up as she watched Damon pace. "This is why I didn't want to say anything. This isn't your problem. It's mine. I can't keep dropping my baggage on you. You have kiddos to protect, and here I am, pushing my way into your life."

Her mind wandered, making up its own narrative when he didn't answer immediately. The taste of defeat stained her tastebuds. She couldn't stay here any longer.

"I believe that's what husbands are for. Well, and other things, but we're not there yet." He winked at her. Her cheeks blushed, not expecting his directness in such a stressful situation. "I love the way we are together. Had that showdown with Brockton never happened at the diner, you'd still be pining away for me, and I'd hate to see you suffer any more than you already have."

She let out an exasperated huff. "Your arrogance is uncanny." He'd a few moments of humor, and she really liked it.

"Is that your way of calling me irresistible?"

"More like incorrigible."

His strong hands wrapped around her. "Does this mean you are the Queen of. . . what's the island called?"

She nodded and shrugged simultaneously. "Summers Island," she stated dryly. "Apparently, people weren't creative, or they wanted everyone to boast about their property.

"Is that all?"

She shook her head. "You'd have to change your last name to Summers. I wouldn't be able to take your surname. I'd never be able to adopt the kids, or they'd have to change their last name to Summers, too." She took another big sigh. "Cheryl may come back demanding money to allow that to happen anyway."

"I have sole custody."

Damon pulled her even closer. Heat spider-webbed down her arms and into her chest. It wouldn't be fair of her to tell him that she loved him. That would weigh into his decision, and she couldn't do that to him.

"The way I see it," Damon stepped his leg between hers. "You have to decide if you want me to be your King, or want another man who is more *king material,* or if you want to let it fall back to your mother. I'll support any decision you make."

For real? Her brows rose.

"Yes. I'll do whatever you ask because. . ." he cupped her cheeks. I am so in love with you; I'd move to your island forever if that's what you want," his voice heavy with emotion.

Joy bubbled inside her like magma threatening to overflow, spilling lava over the entire ranch, wiping it out like it had Pompeii.

"What about the kids? They'd miss their friends here on the ranch."

"I'll pray about it and talk to them."

"You're a smart, sweet, sexy man, you know that?"

"I'll take sexy, but sweet? No." She swatted his arm, and he barely flinched. "Fine, *you* can call me sweet, but don't tell anyone. It'll ruin my image," he joked.

"People already see it, I'm sure."

Clutching the fabric of her pajama shirt in her fist, Harlyn drew in a deep breath. Her own mother's face flashed through her mind. There had been a time when Harlyn cared about helping her mother look like the doting, loving mother she claimed to be. Not anymore. In fact, Harlyn attributed her blunt nature to her upbringing. If people didn't like what she believed or thought, they probably weren't people worth devoting much time to.

"Are you okay? You went somewhere for a minute." He laced their fingers and he guided her to the couch.

"Just thinking about having to always cover for my mother. She wanted everyone to think she was something she wasn't—good, and here you are hiding your goodness, letting everyone see your grumpy or withdrawn side."

"I think you're stretching it a bit. The best of me got washed away eight years ago."

Harlyn belted hushedly, "She got the best of me. She broke my heart, now all that's left is me is beatin' in this guitar. . ." She let the trending country song die off.

"You don't have a guitar, do you?"

"No," he chuckled, wrapping his arm over the back of the couch, his fingertips just barely grazing her shoulder, sending tingles like an electric current down to her fingers.

Harlyn whispered, "Cheryl didn't get the best of you. She lost out on the best years with you. Don't let her take any more of you."

"Thank you," he gently yanked her onto his lap, capturing her lips—first, with a fire that she'd been feeling herself. When her lungs were nearing explosion, he slowed the kiss down, allowing both of them to refill their lungs. He quickly trailed kisses down her cheek to her neck. Not wanting this to end, she let out a frustrated whimper.

His deep chuckle reverberated against her chest. "Someone is over her no-touching rule, eh?"

Harlyn had never imagined she would get to kiss anyone other than the snake Brockton. She was with a kissing master, and he was her husband—another pleasure she never thought she'd have.

Now that she knew what it felt like to be kissed by her man, she couldn't go back.

Chapter 33

"Hey, Damon," Raddix called into the barn. "Can you help me out? At least one of the cows broke through the fence, and I need to wrangle them."

Damon pulled his Carhartt jacket off the peg from the barn wall and zipped it halfway. They'd had snowfall overnight. Damon woke up to Darlene screaming, "It snowed." Her excitement wasn't reciprocated. That might have something to do with the twenty-three-degree temperature. Even now, despite the noonday sun, it couldn't be more than thirty.

All Damon needed to stay warm were recollections of this time with Harlyn this morning.

When he left the bathroom this morning, he watched Harlyn plop back into their warm bed and throw the covers over her head. He knew the transition to winter would be tricky for her.

"Does it have to be so cold?" She'd asked, peeking her head out from under the covers.

"I may not be like Arizona's dry heat, but I can keep you warm if you'd like."

Her mouth dropped. "You are an incorrigible flirt."

They'd grown closer with each passing night, so he knew she was playing along with him. Ever since he'd set his mind on showing her how he felt, things moved in the right direction for them.

"Maybe so, but the offer still stands. I'll see you tonight." He winked at her. Her pink cheeks and shy smile encouraged him to flirt more often.

His mind returned to the present as Damon hopped on Black Jack and raced off to catch up with Raddix."

"Where's your dad this morning?"

"He's at Violet's flower shop."

"How'd things end after their dance?"

Raddix shrugged. "Heck, if I know."

"Maybe he's worried you will be mad."

"I doubt it. I'm glad I'm an adult. He went up one side of me and down the other for that stunt." Raddix huffed out a breath. "I was just an accomplice, but he didn't see it that way."

Damon felt for Sean. Having a wife die must be so much worse than his divorce—he didn't even have feelings for Cheryl, but the agony in Sean's daily expression revealed how much he loved and missed his wife.

Damon could tell by Raddix's expression that he was done with this topic. It must be a dad thing. Damon had asked his kids if they minded that he got remarried, which none of them did—thank God because it had already been a done deal when he asked them.

"Sounds like you might know something about that," Raddix chimed.

"Yeah. My kiddos have accepted Harlyn as their mom."

"Whoa! Back up. What do you mean? Have you fallin' for Harlyn?"

Before Damon could answer, Raddix exclaimed, "Dang, Lily was right. Being married to a psychologist can be useful."

"Yeah, I bet," Damon drawled sarcastically. Those two were so in love with one another that it was sickening.

His phone pinged with a text. Once they reached the bovine escapees, he positioned himself before them, forcing the livestock to turn around and mosey back to where they came from.

He pulled his phone from his pocket to see Harlyn's name in the banner splayed at the bottom of his screen.

I'm holding you to the promise of keeping me warm. This weather is insane.

Are you wearing a coat?

I'm inside!

He laughed out loud.

> **What am I going to get in return?**

Harlyn had surprised him as of late. She knew exactly what he needed, sometimes before he did. Damon found himself rushing through the day to make sure he got as much time as possible with Harlyn at night.

> **You seemed to like the backrub the other night. Maybe that? Unless you decide you'd like something else.**

Was she implying something more intimate? He hadn't pushed her at all. They'd had one great kiss but nothing since. Lately, he'd dreamt of kissing Harlyn in the cabin, the barn, the greenhouse—everywhere, and Lily told him his dreams were reflections of his unconscious desires or emotional needs. She was probably right.

> **Yeah, let's go with the back rub.**

> **Okay. <3**

> **For now. ;)**

The rest of the afternoon flew by. He worked with Tanner and Meadow for a few hours. The NFR was only a month away, but both horse and man were ready. He hoped Tanner and Meadow would bring home gold.

Damon ended his day with his therapy groups. Emmanuel always made his day, even when telling Damon how cute Darlene was.

"Guess what, Damon," Emmanuel asked, sitting ramrod straight on top of Yoshi.

"Dare I ask?"

"What do you mean?"

"Is this something good or bad?" Damon rephrased his question.

"Good for me. Harlyn is coming to my next infusion."

"Come on, Emmanuel." Damon's hands flew in the air. "First, my daughter, now my wife. Is there anything else you want from me?" Damon smiled, but his serious tone confused Emmanuel.

"You're joking, right?"

"Of course I am." Damon led Emmanuel's horse by its reigns. "Pull your shoulders back a little more."

Emmanuel listened. He spent the last five minutes chatting about some Minecraft village he'd created, sporting statues of his favorite superheroes that he built in creative mode.

Damon was familiar with Minecraft only because Reneé used it to teach the kids geometry. Smart. She also had the kids bake when they worked on learning measurements. He appreciated the hard work she put into teaching the kids. Though hers were getting older, Damon hoped Reneé would continue teaching when they graduated.

After saying bye to the other kiddos in the group and their families, Damon and Emmanuel brushed down the horses, and Emmanuel told him how great Harlyn and Lily were for helping out in school today.

"Emmanuel, you're going to dig this."

"What's that mean?"

"You're going to love it," Damon clarified and pulled out Yoshi's halter for the youngster to secure his horse.

"Look at the side," Damon instructed.

Emmanuel knocked some of the alfalfa/grass mix out as he moved it around. Finally, he noticed the patch of his favorite video game character and name hand-stitched on the side.

"Who got me this?"

"Katy taught all the women, but Harlyn did yours."

"Can I go thank her? She's great." Not waiting for Damon's response, the little guy ran off.

He had news for Emmanuel. Damon already knew how great Harlyn was and couldn't wait to go home and tell her that himself.

When he entered the front door, Darlene greeted him with big hugs and shared her day. Dominic and Dean were on the couch doing their homework.

After a few minutes, he asked, "Where's Harlyn?"

"She said she'd be right back. I think she's still in the bedroom."

"Alright. I'll check on her. Why don't you three head up to the main house? We're eating up there tonight."

As he walked down the short hall, feelings he'd kept dormant for so long surged with activity. He couldn't wait to keep his promise and warm up his wife.

He rapped his knuckles on the closed bathroom door as he unbuttoned his flannel and threw it on the floor. "Harlyn, I'm home. I sent the kids up to the main house for dinner. Cash said that it should be ready in about thirty minutes."

No response.

"Harlyn, are you okay?" His undershirt hit the floor, followed by his socks.

He heard the pop of the lock as she twisted the door knob. She appeared red-eyed and blotchy-faced.

Damon arrived in front of Harlyn in an instant with his arms wide. "C-mere. Tell me what's wrong."

She stood frozen and silent.

"You're scaring me; say something," He urged as she stepped into his hug and rested her cheek against his chest. Her tears were wet on his skin, but she warmed the surface of his bare skin like a blanket.

Stop! Now is not the time.

"I've decided to leave. I'm going to the castle to live."

He pulled away from her but didn't let go of her shoulders. "Just you?" The physical and figurative space between them put the Grand Canyon to shame.

Two months ago, this beautiful woman walked into his world and rocked it on its axis. Harlyn backed away even further.

"It's not just Brockton. I got an email from my mother." She pulled out her phone, entered her passcode, and handed it over. The document was still splayed across her screen.

> *Harlyn – I'm coming after you. I'll get what you stole from me. It will be less painful if you return my belongings.*

"She's peachy and to the point." Damon returned Harlyn's phone.

"Nancy Summers doesn't make idle threats."

"Neither do I. Nor do any of the others on this ranch." Damon placed his forefinger below her chin, forcing her to look at him. "I won't accept anything less than the five of us moving to the castle, or we all stay here."

"Damon," she let out an exhausted breath. His stomach flickered at the sweet sound of his name on her lips. Her cute little nose scrunched up, probably trying to think of how to best him in this discussion. She wouldn't. Not this time. She was too important.

"There's nothing you can say to make your leaving okay."

"Fine, tell me why I should stay." her smug tone, raised brows, and smirk triggered Damon's insides.

He stepped closer, feeling brave. "For one," his voice, low and husky, "you're part of the ranch family and this little family of five."

Damon grazed his thumb over her full bottom lip, feeling her tense up. "Second, I can't think about anything other than you. Keeping you safe, playing games with you and the kids, and walking the ranch hand in hand are always on my mind."

His thumb dragged along her bottom lip again. "And kissing you. I haven't been able to think about much else lately."

Her eyes glistened. He wasn't trying to make her cry. In fact, he'd give his left hand if she wouldn't. No such luck. He wiped a stray tear from her cheek. She wrapped her arms around his waist, eliminating all space between them.

"I don't mean to pressure you, but if you're set on moving to the castle, we need to act quickly, and you've seen how my kids move."

She blew out a breathy cry and laughed all at once.

The voice inside his head that always told him the right thing to do wouldn't stop pestering him. *Tell her now.*

He guided her to the couch and settled next to her. "I don't want this to sway your decision; well, maybe I do." She stared at him like he was certifiable. He remembered having the same sweaty underarms and hairline when he told her that he wanted to be her husband for real. That hadn't gone over particularly well, so maybe he shouldn't say anything.

Before the rational part of his brain could shut him up, he exclaimed, "I am in love with you."

Her wide eyes and slacked jaw were not the response he'd hoped for, but in her defense, he had yelled it out rather suddenly.

Before she could say anything, Damon's phone blared from his pocket. "Hold that thought." He fished his phone out, and Raddix's name appeared across the screen.

"We're on our way," Damon answered.

"That's not why I'm calling—we started without you. Have you heard the news?"

"No, what happened?"

"Nancy Summers, heir of Summers International, a conglomerate of some big corporation, was found dead today."

Damon put his hand over the receiver and relayed the information to Harlyn. "What time did you receive that email?"

"Last night, a little after midnight."

He inhaled a deep breath, paused to gather his thoughts, and told Raddix he'd see him in a few right before he ended the call.

With Nancy dead, did that mean Harlyn was free? Immune to having to marry Brockton? Would she ask for a divorce or an annulment? Damon had hoped this day would never come. He loved having Harlyn as his wife, and his kids loved her, too. She supported them in every way—academically and socially. Damon wasn't thrilled that his kids were noticing the opposite sex. Lucky for them, Harlyn was a great buffer.

"Are you okay?" Her dry eyes worried him. Would she let herself grieve? Even though Nancy Summers was controlling and evil, she was Harlyn's mother. Psychologists claim that children will always love their parents, even if they are abusive. It seemed crazy to Damon, but he'd never studied the brain.

"I know I should be sad; she's my mom, but I feel free and want to celebrate my true freedom. I will call Richard and find out what we can do about the castle now."

She playfully shoved him into the bathroom. "Go clean up so we can join everyone."

He stumbled into the bathroom. "I'm going. I'm going."

"Damon." Her sweet voice turned him around. "I love you, too." Her admission lingered in the space between them. His low belly was flint, and her words were the spark, setting his insides ablaze.

"I won't be long. A quick, cold shower should do the trick."

She giggled and threw his dirty shirt and socks at him. He caught them easily and then gently latched the door.

Things were looking up for him. Now, he could start dating his wife and make this real.

Chapter 34

Everyone bid Tanner and Meadow farewell, offering good luck, only to be reminded by the rider himself, "I don't need luck. I have skill."

Damon shook his head and then directed his attention toward Harlyn. "I'll see you back home." He winked at her.

Home. That warmed her heart. She never felt like she had a home. Now she had a great husband and kids to love and who loved her. Harlyn still hadn't shed a single tear for her mother. Was that normal? Probably not. She didn't even feel compelled to get in touch with her dad. He'd left her to fend for herself as a kid. An adult, he can figure things out on his own. That might be harsh, but that's how she stayed happy.

On the way back to the cabin, her heart fluttered. She'd get the kids home and feed them, giving Damon time with his buddy. Then he'd come home to her. The mere thought warmed her from the inside out, welcoming the cool breeze that brushed over her cheeks.

About thirty minutes later, the door flung open. "Grab your coat." The authority in Damon's voice was attractive. "Kids, Harlyn and I are taking a walk on the ranch. Get your homework done, and no fighting."

"I can't get it all done before you get back," Dean argued. "Dad, you need to talk with Miss Reneé. I know high school is challenging, but this is ridiculous."

Harlyn contained her smirk. She was in class with the kids most days and knew how great Reneé was. Dean was just a typical freshman trying to learn the ropes.

"I don't have any homework. Emmanuel and I finished ours before his therapy." Emmanuel's sensory challenges were improving with every session. He still hit himself in the head when his system was overloaded, but the frequency had lessened, especially when Darlene was around.

Dominic looked up from his math work to taunt his sister. "Emmanuel and Darlene up in a tree K-I-S-S-I-N-G. First comes love, then comes marriage—"

"Alright, that's enough!" Damon boomed. "There will be no love, marriage, or anything else in this house."

"You and Harlyn are married." Dean liked challenging his dad on everything, but Harlyn didn't mind this time. She bit the inside of her cheek to keep from laughing.

Harlyn couldn't interpret Damon's granite expression. Had she made a mistake letting him include her in their life? How would she ever leave when this was over? Would he expect her to leave now that her mother was gone and the threat of marrying Brockton was gone?

"Fine, there can be love and marriage for us," Damon waved a hand between him and Harlyn, "but still no babies."

The kids' laughter pulled Harlyn from what she imagined was shock plastered on her face. This was the first time he'd declared his love in front of the kids. Did that mean none of this was pretend anymore?

"Let your brothers finish their work. Why don't you go play."

"Can I go to the main house?"

Damon sighed but agreed, and Darlene was gone.

"You're not going to encourage her to date, are you?" Dean thundered. "You told me I had to be sixteen."

"None of my kids are dating right now." Damon ran his hand through his hair, grabbed Harlyn's hand, and tugged her with him. "We'll be back," he hollered over his shoulder to the boys.

The warmth of Damon's hand over hers heated her entire arm. His large, calloused palm enveloped hers, helping her feel protected and cared for.

"You know, Darlene is good for Emmanuel," her words light, hoping he wouldn't get upset.

"Not again. They're ten." The warmth disappeared when he pulled his hand away.

Oh, well. She wouldn't hold back her thoughts ever again. That was fine if Damon didn't like her opinion, but she wouldn't cower to anyone again.

She conceded, "Agreed, but if they are starting to *notice* each other, isn't it better that you teach them what to pay attention to?"

"I think they'll figure that out on their own," he joked, clearly uncomfortable with the conversation.

She slapped his arm as she spun to face him. Still walking backward, she continued. "You need to teach Darlene to watch how a boy treats his Mama. If he treats her like a princess, he's a keeper; if not, she must run far away unless she's like Nancy. Then everyone needs to run far, far away from her."

"Good point."

"If I could ask your mom how you treated her, what would she say?"

The sadness in his eyes threatened to choke her. "I'm sorry if you don't want to talk about your parents, that's fine."

He straightened to his full height and stared at her with the softest yet wounded eyes, making her heart ache. Reaching for her hand, Damon drew her in until she walked by his side again.

"My parents never wanted me to marry Cheryl. They felt she would break my heart. Clearly, they knew her better than I did." He stuffed his free hand in his pocket.

"Or, they could see her for what she was because feelings didn't blind them."

"Ouch." Damon mocked hurt. "If you're going to keep up with those comments, I'm not going to share," he teased.

She pinched her forefinger and thumb and ran them across her lip like she had zippered them shut.

Damon briefly stared at the worn path before leading her into the orchard.

"Once we had Darlene, Cheryl's true colors started to show. She only cared about the money I made, yet she didn't want me to keep competing. I, of course, assumed it was because she wanted more time with me or didn't want to see me get any more scars." The thought of Damon's scar had Harlyn's blood racing. *Whoa, girl, settle down.*

Guilt riddled Harlyn. She needed to tell him about the money her Grandpa had given her. Being a billionaire was a pretty significant fact he deserved to know. Once he finished his story, she'd tell him.

Damon focused his sights on the ground and blew out a heavy breath. "My last competition awarded me another Gold Buckle and money that Cheryl swindled out of me in the divorce. My mom and dad had traveled to Vegas for this one, sad they'd missed the previous Gold Buckle."

His silence sat heavy on her chest. If only she could take away his pain.

"They took the first flight of the morning the day after. My dad had a doctor's appointment since he hadn't been feeling well. Their plane malfunctioned and landed in a heap, killing everyone."

If that barely-there kiss the other night had landed, their no-touching rule would be so far gone, and she wouldn't feel awkward about wanting to comfort him. Losing loving parents in such a devasting way was horrible.

"It wasn't even two months after that Cheryl told me she'd had an affair with a bronc rider in the same circuit as Tanner and me. She packed up and left."

"Thank God."

"Excuse me?" Damon whipped his head toward Harlyn. "I thought you might pity me. I'm not sure which response is worse."

"It's awful about your parents; I can tell you loved them. But you realize that Cheryl did you a favor, right? There's a woman, somewhere . . ." *like right in front of you* "who will love you the way you deserve. You're the best man I know, Damon Richards, and even if it's only for a little while, some of my fondest memories will always be when I was blessed with the title of Mrs. Damon Richards."

"You don't know many men, do you?"

Well, no, but she wouldn't admit that. The fact that he was the best out of the handful she knew had to count for something.

She bumped his shoulder, missing one apple tree branch as they laughed together. This felt more right than anything else in her life. "I don't give my love out easily."

He didn't respond, making her wonder if she'd said something wrong.

"You better be careful. The lady who wrapped these trees, ooh-wee; she can be pretty harsh. Do you know she even made young children come out and do her job?" She let him change the topic because his teasing lightened the mood.

"Uh," she let out a sassy breath. Halting and plopping her hand on her hip, she squared her shoulders before him. She gently poked her finger into his firm chest. "I'll have you know those *children* offered to help. The man-child I got stuck with was the worst to deal with." A smirk tickled at her lips. But his serious expression grated on her insides.

He wrapped his hand gingerly around her finger. Bringing their attached hands up, he kissed her finger and laced them together. The air between them cracked and sizzled with electricity. Since marrying Damon, her entire world erupted into a love-sick frenzy she couldn't get enough of. Up until now, she'd believed the feelings were one-sided. One could argue, and she had argued with herself many times, that the steamy, smoldering looks and his flirty comments proved he was tired of playing pretend, too, but then something would happen, and his look would disappear.

Kiss me already! There was being a gentleman, but he was taking it a little too far. They were past the no-touching rule. How, after all, could she expect him to keep his hands to himself if she didn't want to reciprocate?

He stepped closer, filling her senses with the mahogany scent booster she'd added to the laundry. She'd never admit she tossed in more than the load required. Talk about reaping the reward of her hard work. His dashing disposition handicapped her nerve endings.

Her breath hitched. "You're special, Damon. Don't let anyone tell you anything different. You're giving Cheryl too much control over your life."

"I don't know about that," his low, raspy voice gave her confidence she had no business having.

"What are you saying?" She slid her hands up his perfectly sculpted arms; with every dip, her fingers lit up like a field of lightning bugs.

He swallowed hard. "What happened to no-touching," he asked without his eyes leaving hers.

She interlaced her fingers behind his neck.

"Harlyn—"

"We're way past that rule," a victorious smirk marked her face. "Besides, the *sort of* kiss the other night was a big letdown. Thought I'd be kind and offer you a chance to redeem yourself."

"Ouch, you go for the jugular. How am I supposed to kiss you now?"

"I'm sure you'll find a way." She massaged his scalp while weaving her fingers through the hair at his nape.

He let out a low growl as he gripped her hips, tugging her flush with him.

"I mean, you are already doing so much for me, keeping Brockton at bay, but now that the situation is under control, you can drop me like yesterday's manure. I want some experience to offer my real husband one day."

Damon looked at her with a strangled expression and clenched jaw. "What makes you think we will end?"

She shrugged her shoulders, not expecting that response. Maybe there was hope of being with this man forever.

He curled his arms around her waist. This close, she saw gold speckles dancing in his hungry eyes. "As far as I'm concerned. I'll be the only one you kiss from here on out."

With an urgency she'd never seen before, Damon captured her mouth. Their lips danced better than Patrick Swayze and Jennifer Grey's characters in *Dirty Dancing*. He tugged at her bottom lip with his teeth, preparing her for the kiss of a lifetime. His hands trailed up her back and deep into her hair as he tilted her head, deepening the kiss. She let out a little moan, her fingers clutched his strong shoulders, hoping this kiss never ended, but knowing it would have to eventually. Much. Much. Later.

As if he could read her mind, he groaned. "Harlyn . . ." he probably wanted to stop; anyone could have been watching.

He picked her up, and she wrapped her legs around his waist. Their mouths twirling together, neither wanted to relent. She whimpered as her head knocked a few forgotten apples from a lower branch.

Guess not.

Harlyn pulled away, laughing. With her chest heaving, she tried to regain oxygen. Any amount would be helpful. She let her feet fall, yet Damon didn't move an inch. He held onto her hips, searching her face; he asked, "Was I still a letdown?"

She ran her fingers across her swollen lips, shaking her head. "I think you just branded me."

Chapter 35

The first week of November in Montana brought even more frigid temperatures. This hadn't bothered Damon, but Harlyn's thin blood revolted. It worked out well for him since Harlyn cuddled more with him and borrowed his sweatshirts, leaving her fruity scent behind for him to enjoy.

Today, that scent enveloped him as they walked hand in hand into the church. He wasn't overly showy, but joy, happiness, and contentment swirled inside him. God brought him and Harlyn together in a round-about way, but that's okay; He knows best.

Damon had been stuck in a private pity party about Cheryl leaving him. He probably wouldn't have pursued Harlyn without God's forceful hand.

The blast of heat smacked Damon in the face when he opened the door for Harlyn. "See why I said dress in layers?"

"Now, this is what I'm talking about," Harlyn said when she entered the sanctuary.

Parishioners were scattered throughout, enjoying pre-service fellowship. The sanctuary buzzed with laughter, revealing the love people in this church had for each other.

"Good morning," Pastor Myles's voice echoed through the sound system.

Harlyn's profile drew Damon in like a fox to a henhouse. He had worried about her since the news of her mother's death. Nancy Summers was pure evil, but he knew Harlyn. She was strong and resilient and holding it all in. Though she hadn't cried yet, Damon figured it would come eventually, and he would be there for her whenever it did.

"How many of you have asked God to forgive your sins?" Nearly every hand reached for the ceiling, including the pastor's.

"How many of you prayed for those who have harmed you?" Not as many hands rose. "In Jeremiah 31:34, the Lord declared, "For I will forgive their wickedness and will remember their sins no more."

Pastor Myles paced back and forth on the stage. "If you are saved, the Lord has forgiven your sins. It's only by His Grace that we are forgiven. How many of you are willing to give up that blessing." No hands rose. "Me either. So let me ask you this. Who am I not to pray for or forgive someone who has wronged me?" He continued to pace back and forth. "Jesus forgave the Romans for their actions on Calvary. If my Savior can forgive his executioners, who am I not to forgive a lesser offense?"

At the end of the sermon, we ended like we always did—in silent prayer. Damon prayed first for Harlyn and for peace to fill her heart. Once he saw her bow her head, he turned to the Lord.

Father, please forgive me for my hardened heart. I've allowed bitterness and anger to take up residency because of my parent's death and Cheryl's living. You've blessed me with Harlyn. Thank you for her. Please don't let me take your blessing for granted. In Jesus' name, Amen.

After the sermon, Harlyn asked to speak with Pastor Myles. Damon hadn't expected things to progress this quickly, but he wouldn't complain. Between Raddix and Quinton, they took Damon's kids home while he waited for Harlyn.

Nearly an hour later, Damon hopped out of the truck when Harlyn and the pastor exited the building. They were still talking, so he leaned his shoulder against the truck's frame, crossed his arms and ankles, and waited.

Pastor Myles waved at Damon as they departed, and he returned the gesture with a head nod. His eyes fixed on Harlyn as she approached. "Are you okay?"

"I'm better than okay. Well, that depends on what you say."

He straightened up. The expression etched on her face had his brain on alert. She embraced him instantly, and he felt her entire body shuddered. Heat swirled through his core. "Talk to me, Sweetheart. Are you upset, happy . . ."

"If you're okay with it. I want all five of us to move to the island for a year. I want you and I to be a real husband and wife."

Damon cupped the silky soft skin on her jaw. She closed her eyes and leaned into his hand, and that undid him. His emotion bubbled over. Bending toward her, he captured her lips. Instantly, he felt weightless, even heaven-bound. His arms engulfed her—first around her waist and then traveled up her back. He could barely concentrate on what he was doing when Harlyn's hands traveled over his chest, creating a trail of fire that radiated to his veins. He deepened the kiss as he pinned her between the truck and himself. He left a succession of kisses across her jaw and down her neck. She rewarded him with goosebumps and a slight giggle when he seized the sensitive spot behind her ear.

Harlyn gripped his shoulders, pulling him impossibly closer. Their lips met again in a fevered match. They traded kiss for kiss, each expressing how deeply they'd fallen in love.

Reluctantly, Damon pulled himself away from Harlyn. This woman had stolen his breath and his heart. He rested his palms on either side of Harlyn's shoulders, thankful for the truck to hold up his weakened legs.

All too quickly, he saw the sweetness from a moment ago fade from her gaze. Fear. Vulnerability. Doubt. Dread. They kidnapped his wife's soul, but he would rescue her from them if it were the last thing he did.

Was she already having second thoughts about staying married to him? He'd do anything she wanted. They could get an annulment and start dating her. As long as he could be with her, that was all that mattered to him.

"Don't leave me now," he heard the fragility in his voice. This was not good. He wouldn't lose Harlyn.

"What if he follows us? What if he hurts everyone here because we leave?"

Serendipitously, the blaring sun now deflated behind the clouds, covering the land with a dull, gloomy ambiance. Similarly, Damon's lungs lost their air, and doom and gloom overshadowed his heart.

"This is right where Satan wants you—doubting God's plan. He brought us together in a unique way. He will keep us together on an island for a year and then wherever He guides us."

Damon hoped his words convinced her to keep hope. When she remained silent, he continued.

"What did Pastor Myles say last week? If you want God to open doors for you, you need to open His word." Damon believed this was one of God's open doors. "Let's head to the ranch and pray with our family."

Chapter 36

"I'm not working with anyone else until Damon comes back," Emmanuel declared at the family meeting after church. Damon's heart melted. The boy widened his eyes and ran his little fingers together faster than Black Jack could gallop. That was the most emotional he'd ever seen Emmanuel, breaking Damon's heart.

Since then, Emmanuel had clung to his side, helping Damon with the horses so he could care for them over the next year while Damon was gone—Emmanuel's idea, not his.

Fortunately, Damon had worked overtime the last few days to finish taming the wild stang, so Raddix and Sean had one less wild horse to worry about busting their fencing and structures. Damon was worried about what he'd do for a year without horses to work with. He'd also miss his groups, but Damon meant it when he said he'd do anything for Harlyn. If living in a castle made her happy, then so be it.

They'd decided it would be best to leave for the castle without a big town send-off if Brockton or his goons were around. The people on the ranch were the only ones who knew of Harlyn's entire situation. They'd be on an island near the Mediterranean Sea in less than forty-eight hours. He'd never lived in a spot with warm temperatures year-round, nor had his kids, but he was excited about this experience.

The sun ruled the day, but the icy chill brought on by the ominous-looking clouds in the early afternoon increased Damon's blood pressure. *Where were Harlyn and Darlene?*

This morning, Darlene had completed her role perfectly, convincing Harlyn she needed some girl time shopping for things a princess would wear. When Darlene asked, the emotion on his wife's face almost made him jealous. Almost. He knew Harlyn rarely took breaks throughout the day so that she could spend the nights with him.

With her mom gone, Harlyn finally had her freedom. They hadn't seen any more signs of Brockton on the property or in town. He probably returned home when the mastermind died—he didn't have anyone to give him orders.

Damon tapped his front jean pocket for the tenth time this morning. Despite the frigid temperature, sweat formed at his hairline.

Dean and Dominic were at home putting up a congratulations banner the kids made in school with Reneé's help. Carolyn and Cash were making Harlyn's favorite dinner—eggplant parmesan. It wasn't his favorite, but knots wrapped around his intestines prevented him from thinking about food.

The women came up with a game similar to hot potato. Katy made a special wooden ball with a hinge on one side for the occasion. It will house the small red velvet box burning a hole in his pocket. Who knew such a small item could cause Damon so much agony? Would she like the design? Is it too big? Small? What about the color? He didn't imagine Harlyn wanting a traditional diamond, but he put small ones on each side of the primary setting, just in case.

They'd play music, and when the music stopped, Harlyn would be holding the ball, Damon would be on bended knee, she'd say yes, and all would be right in the world. That's how it played out in Damon's head. Something that smooth only happened in the movies or books.

There is always room for error. Case in point, Quinton warned Damon about making out in the orchard or anywhere else on the ranch. They'd increased security—put in state-of-the-art cameras—after Lily's stalker snuck onto the property, holding her hostage. He hadn't thought of the cameras, but in his defense, Damon didn't think about anything other than Harlyn.

The sun was determined to fall asleep, leaving streaks of pink and orange in the sky. During the winter months, the sun set early, around four, making people think it was later than it was. Though it was technically early, Damon expected the girls home hours ago. *What could have delayed them?*

Damon's phone buzzed. Pulling it out, he saw a text from Tanner.

I've arrived. Meadow was the star of the corral this morning. Let's hope she can come through in less than a month. We need gold!

She'll do great.

Damon thought of his prep routine when he competed. He'd never left this far in advance of a competition. Tanner relished in the limelight, and that was why he went early.

Too bad you're missing the excitement here.

What?! Don't leave me hanging.

I'm asking Harlyn to marry me.

Aren't you already married? *Laugh/cry emoji*

Funny. For real.

It's about time you replace that cloth ring thing on her finger. Are you getting a ring?

No, I prefer to keep my fingers, thank you. I might get a tattoo ring.

You must really love her.

You know it.

Can someone record it for me?

Sure. Good luck with Meadow. We'll be watching.

He imagined they'd have a television in the castle. Damon wouldn't tell Tanner the situation until after the nationals. Distractions were the worst for a competitor.

"Wish me luck," Damon said as he patted Apple Jack on her neck, and the mare neighed in response. He released a pent-up laugh, making him realize how tense he was. "She's going to say yes," he spoke aloud as he flicked off the lights and secured the barn door. The few ranchhands that resided on the property would check on the animals later.

Damon arrived at the cabin within ten minutes. The boys had outdone themselves. Everything was clean, and the banner looked perfect. Now, all he needed was his wife. "Thank you, boys. It looks great. Head to the main house. I'll shower and be right there."

On his way, Damon texted Harlyn.

> **What time will you and Darlene be home?**

Panic hit him fiercely when he arrived at the main house and still hadn't heard back. Conjured-up thoughts ransacked his head.

Everyone sat around the table, weighing their options. "Maybe we should call Gerard as a friend, and he could give us some direction," Lily suggested.

"On it," Raddix pulled out his phone and stepped away from the table.

Damon's phone rang. "It's Frank's." His eyebrows pinched together. He was the last person Damon expected to hear from.

"What's up, Frank?" Everyone stared at Damon with bated breath.

"Darlene is here."

Damon's body instantly went cold, as if all the blood drained from his veins. *If Darlene is at the diner, where is Harlyn?* Frank continued talking, but Damon stopped breathing. His phone fell from his ear, causing a thud on the table, causing everyone to jump. Sweat dripped down his temples. Katy took control of his phone, and Jeff slapped him on the back like a doctor would slap a baby on the butt at birth to get him breathing. His knees almost gave out on him. Jeff placed his hands on Damon's shoulders, guiding him into the chair. He dropped his hat on the table, forgetting to take it off before he entered the kitchen, and forced his palm heels into his eye sockets. He couldn't hear what Frank was saying, and Katy's words didn't sound encouraging. His leg bounced ferociously up and down until he stood and started pacing with one hand on his hip while the other ran through his hair.

"Do you know how long ago she was taken?" Damon's feet froze, and he grabbed the table.

"Taken? Who? Don't you dare say Harlyn." Damon's voice was deep and full of fear. Fear that he'd never thought he was capable of.

Katy's eyes confirmed his worst nightmare. "You can't be serious!" Damon bolted upright.

"Raddix, tell the sheriff to get to the diner. Someone's taken Harlyn," Jeff ordered.

Sean grabbed the trash can when he saw Damon gag. Presenting in front of Damon mere seconds later, Damon emptied the contents of his stomach into the basket.

He'd finally found someone who loved him as much as he loved her, and now Harlyn had been ripped from him. *Lord, please keep Harlyn safe. Help us find her and keep me from killing anyone.*

"Let's go. We've got to bring your wife home safe and sound." Sean handed Damon his hat as they left for the diner.

"From your lips to God's ears."

Chapter 37

A faint drum beat in Harlyn's head released radiating pain from the bridge of her nose to the base of her skull. Turning her head, her hair matted against her cheek. Why was her hair sticking to her face? Harlyn pried her eyes open, seeing successfully through her puffy or maybe swollen eyes. She moved her stiff jaw to the left, then the right. Had she been hit and not remembered?

The slightly opened window and jarred curtain let in a faint breeze and a string of light. Harlyn attempted to sit up, but all the sinister actions came rushing back.

With one raw wrist trapped inside metal handcuffs, begging to be released, and her feet bound with zip ties to the footboard of the bed keeping her captive, Harlyn lay helpless. She'd worked hard to stay away from Brockton and her parents, yet here she was, back in their grasp. At least Brockton's.

There wasn't anyone else she fathomed would hurt her. She couldn't wait until he showed his grimy face. She'd tell him a thing or two. *What am I thinking? I can't do anything handcuffed.*

Her death warrant was written along the desolate, white walls in a room that reminded her of a hospital. The only things missing were the overwhelming smell of antiseptics and beeping machines. Stale, hot air filled her senses. *At least Brockton gave her a little air from the window.* Situated in the middle of the room, the head of the bed faced the only door; Halryn wiggled, releasing her sweat-ridden legs from the sticky sheets as she pondered her options, disappointment perched on her chest, determined to keep her captive.

Fear saturated her inside and out. Hopefully, Darlene was able to get into the diner safely. Maybe help would be here before she knew it. More questions riddled her hurting brain. How long had she been confined to this room? What had they given her? With a headache the size of Montana, she assumed it was powerful enough to subdue her for hours.

Doubt seeped in. If Brockton had been behind this, they would have been in a more luxurious place. He judged every place by its appearance. Her free hand was a lead weight. Harlyn's captor obviously didn't deem her a flight risk if he didn't subdue all her limbs. Whatever they knocked her out with, still had her arm enslaved.

A closer study revealed blood laced on her fingertips. A tear slinked down her face as reality sunk in. Her hair soaked into her bloody face. Why was it bloody?

All she could remember was seeing Brockton in his Benz. Despite Darlene's resistance, she finally listened to Harlyn and ran toward the diner.

"Hide in the woods. Don't move. Wait forty minutes for these goons to clear out and head to the diner."

"I don't have a watch." Harlyn pulled her Apple watch from her wrist, securing it to the little girl's. "Go. Don't look back."

Brockton pulled Harlyn from her motorhome, dragging her toward his car, but she didn't remember getting in. A jab pierced her arm and the base of her skull. Then everything had gone black. Now, she was in this shabby room, alone. Maybe that was not all bad. She didn't want to see anyone. Figuring a way out of this was her only goal.

Lord, I trust you have a plan because I don't. Please make sure Darlene is okay and get her back to Damon. Your will be done on Earth as it is in heaven. Please give me the strength to endure whatever you have planned for me.

Faint creaks from the hallway burned her ears.

Goodbye, freedom. Hello, prison or, God forbid, death.

A few seconds passed. She held her breath, filled with uncertainty until the door flung open. In front of her stood a tall, lanky, shrewd-looking man with sneaky dark eyes that roamed over the length of her body. *Dear God, please keep him away from me.*

If someone had told her yesterday that she'd wish for Brockton's presence, she would have laughed in their face. The one thing her mother always said came rushing back and rang true—*"Never say never."*

The breath she'd been holding came out in an icy snarl. "What bar did you just stumble out of?"

He made slow, deliberate steps toward Harlyn—real predator-prey-type stuff only seen in the movies and books. When had her life turned into entertainment? The slimeball reeked of alcohol and sweat.

Nerves bounce in her stomach as jolts of awareness stab at her mind, and she silently begged, *please don't rape me. Start fighting, Harlyn*, her mind ordered.

"I don't know who you are, but someone put you up to this. Whatever amount they promised you, I can give you more if you let me go."

A sinister chuckle escaped the drunk's lips. "They didn't promise me money." His eyes roamed over her in a sleazy, slimy way, inching even closer.

"Get out here," a female voice demanded from beyond the partially opened door.

The drunk guy winced and left as quickly as he could, stumbling over himself in true drunk style.

Harlyn couldn't hear clearly, but that voice sounded familiar to her.

"Do not touch her. You are supposed to make sure she gets her food and water, nothing else."

Wait . . . What is happening? A woman was keeping her hostage yet still willing to feed her. None of this made sense. This was a sick joke. She'd freed herself from her controlling, manipulative parents and remained out of Brockton's hands for the last ten years, and now someone else is calling the shots? She'd seen Brockton right before everything went black. Where was he now?

Her parched throat tightened as she tried to speak. Unfortunately, she'd released her bodyguards too soon. No one would have taken Harlyn if she'd listened to Richard and Stan and kept them. She had the money for them, but that wasn't the issue. She'd been sick and tired of having them follow her around. She felt terrible for their families—they'd dedicated much of their lives to her safety. Guess hindsight is twenty-twenty.

Once she arrived on the ranch, she felt like she'd made the right decision. Harlyn felt safe and part of a family that she enjoyed and wanted to be around. Almost like another universe. On the ranch, she was married to the most handsome cowboy.

A wave of emotion crashed through her like a tsunami of lost opportunities, crushing her soul. They were leaving for the island. She planned on adopting the kids and being their mom. They've already been through so much since Cheryl left them. *Please, Lord, let me return to them.*

Nausea blasted in her stomach. Maybe that woman outside her door would keep her safe from the scumbag touching her, but there was no way she'd eat anything anyone gave her.

The whispers were getting more faint. Why were they leaving her? She wanted answers. Harlyn flinched when the door slammed closed, cutting her off from whoever was on the other side of the door.

Clearly, she wasn't getting answers right now.

Chapter 38

Snow showers began to fall while Gerard was questioning Darlene in the diner. Winter was her favorite month, so when the snow didn't distract her in the slightest, everyone knew how much the situation had shaken the little girl.

Damon appreciated Lily's presence during the questioning. She could help this go smoother. Nothing against Gerard, but he didn't have Lily's skillset.

"How many people did you see?"

She swirled her straw around her milkshake. "There were at least six. They were old and men."

"Old?"

'Yeah, at least thirty."

Everyone laughed since Lily had just turned thirty and was the next youngest adult on the ranch.

"I must have one foot in the grave, according to your little Cherub," Hazel joked with Damon.

"How many vehicles were there? Do you remember colors?"

"The one they dragged Harlyn to was a black one with like a peace sign in the middle between the headlights."

All of the adults looked at each other with confused looks.

"Can you draw it for us?" Lily asked.

Gerard handed the girl his pen and paper when she shook her head.

"I remember this from fractions." She drew a circle and divided it into thirds.

"A Mercedes Benz," Katy gasped. I saw it that night at the diner." Every adult knew she was referring to the night Brockton invaded their town.

"Good. Now. Where were you when this happened?"

"Haven't you seen her motorhome?"

They had. Gerard found it abandoned. He wanted to make sure the answers all lined up. Confusion happened with people in traumatic situations; he didn't want to follow the wrong lead. At first, Damon was annoyed by the sheriff's insinuation that Darlene would give him false information. However, Damon realized Gerard didn't mean anything toward Darlene in particular; everyone struggled after being in a dire situation. He didn't want to slow the sheriff down, so he let him do his job.

The sheriff questioned Darlene for another twenty minutes, gathering pertinent information. He conversed with the state police. They shut down the roads most likely used for a quick getaway, broadcasted an APB, and contacted all the local hotels, motels, and Inns. They couldn't have gone too far but needed to find her quickly.

As they left the diner, the snow showers had turned into a snow squall. Fortunately, Quinton and Amelia were at the ranch with Carolyn and Cash. Though Amelia has been working with Lily to overcome her intense fear of storms, she was still a work in progress.

Damon followed Gerard in his truck while Katy and Jeff took Darlene home. They headed back to where he'd found her motorhome. Would Harlyn be upset that it was gone? They'd set it ablaze, probably hoping she hadn't found the map and paperwork informing the world that Harlyn owned an island and castle. Fortunately, Richard and Stan both had copies in any unfortunate event.

When they arrived, blue and then white lights on the back of the police-issued Explorers blinded Damon as he weaved between vehicles toward the burnt motorhome home. Dozens of police officers donned winter jackets, knit hats, and gloves scoured the area, looking for any evidence that might lead to the kidnappers' whereabouts. The relentless snow would discourage most people, but not these men and women. Winter was just beginning in Montana, which may be just the advantage they needed.

"Sheriff, look at this," an officer from the next town over called to Gerard. Damon had seen the man before but couldn't remember his name.

The officer handed Gerard a device he'd found under the burnt-out hood. "Nice work," Gerard slapped the young officer on the back, bestowing upon him a rare smile.

"Thank you, Sir."

Gerard was a great guy, but he rarely smiled in uniform. Unless, of course, he spotted Willow. Damon recalled the night at the dance hall he'd been called when Brockton's goons tried to thump Damon and Tanner.

"What's that?"

Gerard held it up. "A tracker."

"That's how he kept finding her," Damon's realization hit hard. "But Harlyn told me that her bodyguards found trackers and removed them early on."

"Those might have been decoys or backups. This was on the engine, so unless it needed work, they wouldn't have thought to look there."

A trail of half-covered footprints caught Gerard's attention. "Follow me, Damon. You have your handgun?"

"Definitely," Everyone on the ranch carried, knowing they could encounter dangerous wildlife at any moment."

"Don't take it from your holster unless I tell you to."

Two other officers fell in line behind Damon.

"Blood at three o'clock, Boss." Everyone's head turned to the right. A piece of a bloody shirt hung from a tree limb."

"Could this be a trap?" Damon asked. "Maybe they are intentionally wasting your time to keep you from finding Harlyn."

Gerard stopped short. Damon first noticed the frown on the sheriff's face. Then he pressed a button on the side of his phone and spoke into it. "I need a medic about five hundred feet northwest of the scene."

Everyone followed the sheriff, who picked up his pace. They stopped when the trail of blood led to a body slumped in the snow. They ducked under low-hanging branches and leaped over rotted tree stumps. Damon's feet were set beside the man's body. He felt terrible for the man with his face buried in the snow, but at least it wasn't Harlyn. *Thank you, Lord."

Gerard turned the man over; shock hit him like a punch in the gut. Gerard felt the man's neck. "He has a pulse. It's weak, but there."

"If Brockton is here, who has Harlyn?" Damon asked, not bothering to hide his frustration.

Brockton tried to free his lips, like the Tin Man in the Wizard of Oz when he first met Dorothy. Gerard and Damon knelt in the snow, and the words that came out of his mouth fell like lead in Damon's stomach.

"Nancy's alive."

Chapter 39

Her stomach rumbled like thunder on a spring day, and her head ached, threatening faintness. The smell of bacon coated the room. The slimeball had brought in a BLT sandwich, chips, and water with lemon hours ago. He'd set it on the bed near her free hand and told her she'd have eggplant parmesan for dinner.

Whoever took her knew her favorite meal choices. About five minutes ago, when the sandwich tempted her to eat it like the Devil did Jesus on the mountain during Jesus' forty days of fasting, she tossed the plate like a frisbee, hitting the wall.

She closed her eyes and saw Damon looking back at her. His eyes hypnotized Harlyn and drew her in like gravity to the center of the Earth. His fierce, protective nature had saved her from Brockton at the diner. Could he save her again? Meanwhile, she remained tied up, stripping her dignity from her second by second.

A renegade tear fell without her permission. She hadn't cried since she was three years old. She swiped at her cheek, not about to let the Devil get to her now. *"Crying showed weakness,"* her parents drilled into her head. Though she didn't believe that, she imagined the people who held her might, and weakness was the last thing she wanted to show.

The same slimeball entered the room, a string of curses coming from his lips. "If he'd done his job, I wouldn't be in this problem," he mumbled as he walked toward her.

"Tell me who you're working for!"

His lips slowly spread into a sinister smile, letting her know he wouldn't tell her anything. "The next part of the plan will reveal everything you need to know."

She nodded to appear compliant. However, right now, she wanted him to leave so she could plan her escape. Nothing came to mind except to break the balusters on the bedpost. He'd return and probably tie up her free hand if she made too much noise.

The sound of breaking glass radiated through the open door.

"What's going on?"

He cursed. "Someone else must not have done their job. She gets crazy when that happens."

"Why doesn't *she* come in and explain what *she* wants from me?"

His menacing laugh made Harlyn cringe on the inside. "She won't let you see her and live to tell about it. She doesn't want to kill you, so it's best you don't see her."

"None of this makes sense. I thought Brockton was the one who captured me. He's the only one sick enough to do this now that Nancy's dead."

The drunk's terrorizing snicker cut Harlyn in half. "To ease your mind, I'll share what I came to tell you." He stepped closer, causing Harlyn's stomach to revolt. She swallowed to clear the bile rising in her throat. "Brockton didn't follow orders quick enough; he's dead in the woods near your fried motorhome, and your mom is not dead, just another part of the boss's brilliant plan."

"Who is your boss."

"That's all for now. Hang tight until I have more orders."

Her bones started to freeze, but she was afraid to say anything; who knew what this deranged person was capable of? Harlyn searched her brain. Who would want to harm her besides Nancy or Bill? The boss is a woman—Harlyn didn't know any woman from her past who didn't like her.

She wrapped her hand around the post in the headboard and wiggled it with all her might. The faint cracking sound gave her a burst of hope and energy. Using her free hand, too, she snapped the wood, freeing the handcuff from the wood piece.

How would she free her feet now? Fortunately, she was flexible because it wasn't that easy to be spread eagle and use enough leverage and force to break the balusters on the footboard. A crashing sound radiated through her room when she broke one foot free. *Please, God, give me the strength to free myself before they come in here. Then give me the wisdom to get out of here, know where I am, and get back to the ranch.*

Using her free heel, she only needed one strong kick, and her other foot was free. Footfalls heading her way caused her anxiety to peak. "What do I do?"

Grab the wood and hide behind the door.

Harlyn did as her brain directed, which reminded her of a police show she watched in which one detective had to free her boss.

The door flung open, and the drunk swore when he saw the empty bed. Before he could call for help, Harlyn jumped on his back with the piece of wood crammed against his throat. She squeezed her legs around his waist for all she was worth and pulled back on the wood, hoping he'd lose consciousness soon.

No such luck.

He rammed his body against the wall, knocking the wind from her. Maybe this plan wouldn't work. No wonder Lily told her to watch some actor named Jason Statham, who said his moves from a movie she saw saved her from her stalker. Too late for that now, as he rammed her against the wall again.

She didn't need that actor; she had God. *Lord, please give me the strength of Sampson to put this man down. Better yet, snap and wipe out all these people and set me free. Close the lioness's mouth and let me be safe here until Damon finds me. You're capable of anything; please help.*

The brute rammed her a third time. Just as she felt her strength slipping away, the man fell to the floor.

"Thank you, Lord," her breathless adoration for her Savior never faltered. Now, was there a way out of this house? She picked up the same piece of wood and peered out the door and down the hall.

Her eyes checked both ways before she entered the empty hallway. Faint voices grew louder as she stalked toward what she assumed would be an exit.

"If all you want is money, what are you waiting for? Go insist she give it to you."

That voice. No, it couldn't be.

"And you think she's going to hand over a billion dollars? She probably doesn't even have control of that money. From what you said, Harold was savvy. He probably planned every bit for her. How do you suggest we get her to have whoever is in charge of her money hand it over?"

"Harold was smart, but my daughter is not. She got rid of the bodyguards like I told you she would. With Harlyn, you must have patience."

Her heart poured like soup onto the floor. She knew her father wasn't any better than Nancy, but this was another level. Who is the woman? That voice sounded so familiar, but she'd been out of her childhood world for so long she couldn't place it.

When her dad went away for those long trips, was he meeting with this woman? The boss, as the drunk called her? Did these two have anything to do with Nancy's death? Grandpa left her a million dollars. Had they already wiped Nancy clean?

Harlyn's breath hitched when the cold steel barrel of the 9mm pressed against her temple. "Move." The drunk recovered too quickly. Harlyn should have tied him up with what she didn't know, but now she was in another precarious position and meeting "the boss" who wouldn't let her live once she'd seen her.

"Look what we have here, Boss."

"Rosalind," Harlyn spoke barely above a whisper.

"You didn't strike me as a wimp, Butch. How did this little thing overpower you?"

He opened his mouth to answer and snapped it shut when the least likely person narrowed her eyes at him.

"I don't understand. You were nice to me," Harlyn said, directing her comments toward Brockton's mom.

The cunning smile on the evil woman's face made Harlyn sick. "You were easy to be nice to, but it's been a while. How do you think it will go now?"

"Have you been having an affair with Brockton's mom since I was a teenager?" Harlyn directed her question at her dad.

"You know, the funny thing about Harold. . . he called me numb or oblivious, but I knew he'd pull everything and give it to you. The million dollars he left Nancy was a slap in the face."

Her arm was starting to lose circulation where Butch, as Mrs. Jenkles called him, gripped her. "Unless you call off the brute, I will lose my circulation, and then you get nothing from me."

"You're a fighter now, are you?" Bill asked condensedly.

"You bet I am, *Dad*. You can't control, manipulate, or hit me into compliance anymore."

"We'll see about that."

Lord, please don't let these monsters win.

"Did you two kill off Henry, too?" Harlyn had a sick feeling that they killed her mother. Not that there was any love loss for the woman, but taking a life not in self-defense is wrong.

"Set her in that chair, Butch, but keep the gun on her," Rosalind ordered.

He shoved her down. She was surrounded by evilness. How could she let her light continue to shine?

"It's best you don't ask questions, Dear. The more you know, the higher your chances of being killed."

"Where's Brockton?" Harlyn ignored the woman's warning.

"Are you inept, or trying to irritate me?"

Harlyn shrugged. "I think it's only fair to know what fate I should expect."

Henry couldn't run a business if he tried, yet he wanted to make all the decisions and let people think he knew what he was doing. On the other hand, Brockton was smart and could have grown our family business, making us filthy rich. Except, Henry lost it when you ran off, taking our two hundred million dollars with you." Harlyn's eyebrows climbed, then she shook her head and narrowed her eyes at Rosalind. "Our dowry, Dear. Keep up."

Keep her talking; help will show up. Peace fell on Harlyn at that moment.

"Henry disowned Brockton, and our business started to fail. That's when Bill informed me that Nancy had been paying Brockton to keep tabs on you."

She'd stopped telling me her plans when she suspected Rosalind and I were having an affair. We hadn't been, but it was an idea that grew roots. She divorced Henry, and I strung Nancy along to keep tabs on you, my sweet daughter."

"Long story short," Rosalind interrupted. "I contacted Brockton and paid him to bring me information about you. Nancy didn't like that she was losing ground. She confronted Bill and me, things got heated, and I eliminated her."

"Let me get this straight, you killed my mother because you wanted to find me, and you didn't like that she was questioning why you were sleeping with her husband?"

"So, where's your double agent son now?"

Nonchalantly, she twirled her fingers in the air. "He's probably dead in the woods where we took you."

"What?! Who killed him?"

"He was trying to escape with you. I had a feeling he was double-crossing us, and I couldn't have that," Bill declared.

"You let him kill your son?" Rosalind shrugged. Harlyn was in the Twilight Zone.

"Now, tell us where the island is and give us access to your offshore accounts, and we'll let you go," Rosliand said like she was ordering lunch at a restaurant.

"How do you know about the castle?"

"I was supposed to be the King." Bill clenched his jaw, putting Harlyn on alert. "All the money inside the castle goes to the husband. It would have been mine, and I guarantee there's more in the castle than you have in any account, so I don't care about your accounts; I want to know where the castle is." Bill's face matched that of a stop sign. He narrowed his eyes at her as he took one meticulous step after another in her direction. His flaring nostrils meant he was ready to strike.

'Your mother was good until she met your father.' Her grandpa's words ran through her mind. He was the problem all along. Had her mother been so miserable that she lost her way and took it out on Harlyn? He controlled her so much that she forgot who she was. Is that why her grandparents never gave up on her mother? But hadn't Nancy killed her own mother? Tears of frustration threatened to overflow. *Be strong, Harlyn. This is not the time.*

"I don't need you to get that map. I just figured you'd rather I take my aggression out on you and not that sweet little girl you were with earlier."

"You stay away from her!" Bill pushed Harlyn back down in her chair like she was a mere feather. *Shoot, shoot, shoot. I gave him leverage. Lord, please protect everyone at the ranch, especially Darlene.*

A flash of movement out the window caught Harlyn's attention. She lifted her chin and stared at her dad so she could use her peripheral vision. Her heart leaped when she realized the police were there to save her. *Keep them talking.*

"Since you don't want my money, I could be convinced to give you that castle and island."

Chapter 40

"How much longer do we have to wait?" Damon asked. "Don't you have enough dirt on them to bust in there and arrest all three of them?"

Damon wondered if anyone inside this abandoned house knew the police owned it. The cameras and audio captured everything they needed to convict Harlyn's dad and Brockton's mom.

Once the medics put a tourniquet above the gunshot wound in Brockton's leg and gave him some fluids, he was able to tell Gerard that Butch, his mother's bodyguard shot him in the leg. But more importantly, he led the police to Harlyn when he informed them that Nancy was locked up in a shed at an abandoned house on Wilson Road.

Based on how lax Butch was holding the gun at Harlyn, Damon didn't think the bodyguard was worried about keeping his position.

"We need to wait for the clincher."

Just then, an officer released a woman Damon presumed was Harlyn's mother. She walked past him barefoot in the snow in a torn and tattered dress. She stormed through the front door, and he heard a shriek from inside.

"You were dead!"

"That's what you thought, Rosalind," Nancy glared at the woman with laser focus like Superman. Damon looked away, able to feel the heat through the window from her glare.

"Shoot her!" Rosalind screamed at no one in particular, but Butch held the only visible gun. He kept that focused on Harlyn, so Bill pulled one from behind his back—

"Breech!" Gerard roared into his phone, and every officer moved with precision.

"Butch is taking Harlyn out the back," Damon called, running in that direction. He had his gun drawn and pointed at the door as Butch barreled through it.

Pointing the gun at Harlyn's head and increasing the pressure of his forearms around her neck until she winced, Butch ordered Damon to back off.

"Let her go, and I will. I don't care one iota about you, so that means you can walk free, or I can kill you where you stand."

"Keep dreaming," Butched pushed out a breathy laugh, taunting Damon.

Damon fired, and Harlyn shrieked as the bullet whizzed by Butch's ear. "Now, you might think I'm a bad shot, or I might have intentionally made that bullet zoom by your earlobe as a warning. Are you a gambling man?"

"I'm not going to jail. Anything I ever did was because that woman threatened to kill my mom. She's got MS, and I needed money for her treatments and home healthcare."

Damon kept his gun steady on Butch's forehead. He could take the man out right now but didn't want to unless he had to, especially if he was a victim in Rosalind and Bill's charade. "I'm sorry about your mom. I don't care what you've done. I only care about what you will do with Harlyn in your arms."

Gerard appeared on the west side of the property with his gun fixed on Butch. "It's over, put the gun down."

Butch turned abruptly, taking away Damon's shot. Harlyn stared at him with pleading eyes.

Don't worry. We'll save you, Damon mouthed.

The windows rattled when two gunshots went off inside the house.

"Report," Gerard commanded into his phone, waiting for a response.

"Fatal shot, Sir, to one of the accused."

Gerard resumed his work with Butch. "Did you hear that? One of the people you worked for is dead. Do you want that same fate—"

"Or do you want to see your mom again," Damon questioned, hoping it was the leverage they needed for him to free Harlyn.

"I'm not the bad one. I needed the money for my mom," Butch tried to argue.

"Let her go, nice and easy. Tell us everything you know, and we'll let the judge know that you cooperated. You might be able to see your mom again."

Gerard was more patient than Damon. He'd wanted to shoot the man at least five times in the last few minutes. He wouldn't have shot to kill, but he wanted Harlyn back.

"Come on, Butch, I'm going to lose my patience."

Ah, he is human.

"You won't shoot me with her here."

"Don't tempt me," Gerard warned.

Oh, no. Lord, help Gerard keep his patience, or please guide the bullet away from Harlyn if he shoots.

Damon's lungs burned with anticipation.

"Nothing you could do to me would be worse than what that man standing over there would do if anything happened to the woman in your clutch. I don't have anything on you right now, but if something happens to her, you're going down one way or another."

Butch's eyes darted back and forth between Gerard and Damon.

"Come on, Man. Release her and drop to your knees," Gerard ordered more forcefully.

"Think about your mom. She won't be able to see you behind bars. Let her go," Damon's voice pleaded, concern laced in every spoken word.

His grip on Harlyn's throat slowly released until he dropped his arm completely. Harlyn ran to Damon, who hugged her tight with one arm while he kept the gun fixed on the man until Gerard had him in cuffs.

"Thank you so much. God told me you were coming for me. Well, someone was coming. I'm so glad you're here." She squeezed her arms around his neck briefly before pulling back. "Is Darlene okay?"

He shook his head. "She's fine." Harlyn cried. He'd never seen that before, and it about crushed his ribcage, leaving his heart unprotected and vulnerable to attack.

Gerard walked a cuffed Butch by Harlyn and Damon. "Wait, Sheriff." Harlyn moved toward Butch. He stared at her, bracing himself.

"I'm sorry I attacked you, but I had to get free."

Butch shook his head. "You have nothing to be sorry for. I am sorry. I hope I didn't hurt you."

"You knocked the wind out of me—"

"I'll kill you!" Damon rushed forward.

Gerard positioned himself between Damon and the criminal.

"I'm fine now," Harlyn said, stopping Damon by placing her palms on his chest.

"I'd like to make sure your mom has the money she needs for her treatments; that way, you can spend whatever remaining time she has left together. Please give the sheriff her address and phone number, and he'll get it to me. Stay out of trouble, Butch.

Color spilled across Butch's face. Damon knew Harlyn had a way of making people realize their wrongdoings. Hopefully, the shame he felt right now would be enough to keep him out of trouble later.

"Thank you, Harlyn." Gerard led the man away.

Damon wrapped his arms around his wife's waist from behind. "Let's go home. Everyone wants to see you."

And Damon couldn't wait to propose.

Epilogue

Three snowstorms later, Harlyn reveled in her engagement ring. The cute game they played, Damon's handsome face looking up at her, and her favorite meal once she said yes were blessings after the ordeal with the people from her past. She still hadn't processed everything, but fortunately, she had Lily. The woman was a great listener. She only had two virtual clients, and Emmanuel, so Harlyn offered Lily enough money to be the official counselor for the ranch.

Amelia had mentioned doing that, and Harlyn begged Amelia to let her take care of Lily's salary. Not that Amelia couldn't afford it; she was a millionaire herself, but Harlyn knew her desire was selfishly motivated—to talk with Lily often in the hopes she'd heal quicker.

Gerard was true to his word after Butch cooperated. He received five years probation and no jail time. Gerard told her that his sentence had more to do with Harlyn's testimony and her desire to help his mom. Since Butch hadn't killed anyone, shooting Brockton in the leg instead of eliminating him, the judge believed the man's story and gave him a second chance at making a good life for himself.

Rosalind Jenkles had lied. Henry's company wasn't failing due to his inept skills; she embezzled the money right out from under him. Her controlling and manipulative actions led him to believe he was worthless, causing him to give up. In the end, she killed him anyway. Halryn wondered if he'd started to see the light and confronted her.

Bill Summers's funeral was yesterday. Harlyn didn't know who attended, nor did she care. Nancy Summers avoided jail time because she hadn't killed anyone in cold blood. Cameras inside the house revealed that Bill slid out of the zip ties used to pin his arms behind his back. As Bill reached for an officer's gun, Nancy shot him twice and put the gun on the floor. She didn't resist arrest after that. The judge declared her a considerate citizen, not allowing Bill to kill anyone else.

Harlyn didn't know what to think. The words considerate and Nancy Summers were never in the same sentence before, but Harlyn had learned so much in the last few days. How much of it was true? No clue. Harlyn didn't go out of her way to reunite with her mother either. Not yet. She had too many scars to ignore.

Once news reports revealed the brevity of the situation, Harlyn contacted Winnie. Growing up, Winnie was her only friend; She'd never seen Winnie as a housekeeper. Everyone else had either died or moved on when Bill and Nancy disappeared.

"Can you come stay with me now?" Harlyn asked, gripping the phone and bracing for Winnie's response.

"I'd love to. I have something to give you."

Harlyn picked Winnie up from the airport three days later and brought her back to the ranch. She immediately got along with Cash and Carolyn, who requested her assistance in the kitchen. It was a smart choice; Winnie was the best, and the kids loved her just like Harlyn did as a kid and had never stopped.

That night, she sat with Damon and Harlyn in their cabin.

"What's this?" Harlyn asked as Winnie handed her a locked box.

"Open it up with that," Winnie said, pointing to her necklace.

Harlyn studdered, "B-but how can the key open this and the compartment in the motorhome?"

"Your grandparents were brilliant people."

The cold metal burned through Harlyn's jeans. The key easily opened the lock. More papers. Harlyn wasn't sure she could handle any more. They still hadn't decided what to do about the castle. When she finally spoke to Richard again, he told her to keep praying and wait for God's answer. He assured her that everything would work out how it was supposed to if she was patient. *Be still.* She was back to that again.

She opened the first paper.

Dear Harold,

Please don't let this fall into the wrong hands. Mrs. Summers did not kill your wife. Mr. Summers made me give a particular glass to Mrs. Summers and ordered me to spill a different water on your wife. He told me that your wife needed medicine that she refused to take, and that was the only way you'd been successful. I was new, and I know that is not an excuse, but I didn't have a reason not to believe him. I am very sorry.

-Emma

Tears ran down Harlyn's cheeks.

"Emma went missing two days later and still hasn't been found," Winnie said brokenheartedly.

"That poor girl and her family."

Harlyn pulled the final paper from the box.

Hello, my Darling Granddaughter,

This is it. If you've found this, just about everything has been revealed. The last thing you need to know is that your mother was a victim in all of this, at least in the beginning. She should have never married your father. We tried to stop her, but she said she was in love. We knew he only wanted the family inheritance.

I've left everything you to, so you can keep it all. Before you decide, I want to share a little story with you. When your mother was a child, she lived in our Florida place all summer. She pretended she was the princess and the cowboys were her princes, trying to save her from an evil man. Sadly, her pretend world became reality.

Every day, your mother talked about moving to the island with her cowboy prince and living there forever. When she met your father, we knew he had ill intentions, so we adapted the by-laws, and the moment you were born, we gifted it to you. I'm sure you've read the by-laws at this point. You must live there for a year; then you can come and go. If you do not spend the year there, it will return to your mother. She will need to follow the by-laws precisely, and when she passes on, it will become yours again.

Talk with Richard and Stan. If you have a husband, discuss it with him too. I trust you to make the decision that makes you happy.

Love you – Grandpa

Tears ran from her eyes like a faucet. "I'm happy right here. I don't care about having a castle or an island like she did." Turning to Damon, she asked, "Are you okay if the island goes to my mother until she dies? Then we can have a chance at the castle."

"As long as I have you, I don't care where we live, but I'm a little excited that we're staying here so the kids have their friends, and I can still work with the horses."

"It's settled then. I'm going to bed. See you kids in the morning." Winnie bunked in with Darlene for tonight. They hadn't made any long-term plans for Winnie, but they would so Harlyn would enjoy as much time with her as possible.

"Why didn't you tell me that you wanted to stay?" Harlyn's voice was delicate as an orchid.

"That's why. You always care about others before yourself. I wanted to do that for you. If you wanted to live in a castle, we would have. Darlene might be disappointed that she won't be a princess."

"She's wrong. She's our princess." The adoption papers were processed faster than ever in human history. Harlyn believed the judge influenced his judge friends to move the adoption along. But now, Darlene, Dominic, and Dean were legally hers.

"I love you, Damon Richards. I love you, too, Harlyn Summers-Richards. I hate the hyphen, but if Darlene wants that princess title someday, it's how it must be."

Harlyn pressed a lingering kiss on Damon's lips. "You are the best dad ever. As far as fake husbands go, I think you're pretty amazing, too."

"Just wait until the real thing, Sweetheart."

"I'm counting the days." He kissed her with reverence. He'd been there to protect and support her. Now, her picture-perfect husband was even more. He was her future, and she was his. Whatever God put in their lives, they would conquer it together.

Thank you for reading Damon and Harlyn's story. I drank in their banter, convenient marriage, love for the kids, and their growing feelings toward one another. Willow and Gerard's story is next. The Perfect Sheriff will come out in 2025. I am only a few chapters into it, which may become a two-for-one book. Sean and Violet are worming their way into the story. That said, I don't have a preview for you because things are changing rapidly in Haven Ridge, Montana. Stay tuned for more updates regarding your Big L' Ranch friends.

Keep reading, and you'll find chapter one of When the Dust Settles: A Sweet Romance with a Navy SEAL. G & G Security, my new series with these characters crossing over, will be released in 2025.

How About a Review?

Your feedback is valuable, so please consider sharing your thoughts. This will help other readers discover this book and my other works.

Thank you from the bottom of my heart for reading and reviewing my book(s).

Amazon

Goodreads

Bookbub

Acknowledgements

"And whatever you do, in word or deed, do everything in the name of the Lord Jesus, giving thanks to God the Father through him." —Colossians 3:17

It is a privilege to write and share my stories with the world. I do not take the responsibility lightly, and it's not something I could do on my own.

Thank you to my family, who encourages me and helps me edit. Thank you to all the people who dare share stories with me and allow me to use them as inspiration and excitement for each story I pen.

To Laura, thank you for providing the necessary feedback to improve the reader's experience; I know they are as grateful as I am for your honesty. To all my ARC readers, thank you for spreading the word about my book. Your time reading, reviewing, and posting comments is invaluable.

About the Author

Karen Tucci, a public school teacher by profession, now tutors writing students online and homeschools her two children.

A native of Maine, she has trekked miles of the Pine Tree State and visited countless others. It is through her life experiences that the basis for her romance stories develop. One of her favorite things to say when out adventuring is, "...that is definitely going in my next book!"

Fun fact: Karen had only read and wrote non-fiction growing up. It wasn't until her late twenties that she embraced the joy brought forth by doing both — reading and writing — within the different romance tropes. Now, she reads at least fifteen fiction novels a month and writes daily!

Connect with Karen:

Facebook Reader's Group.

To find out about special deals, giveaways, and new releases, join her newsletter:

https://www.trueheartromance.com

Instagram

Goodreads

Bookbub

Amazon

Chapter 1 – When the Dust Settles: A Sweet Romance with a Navy SEAL

Grady

Grady Gunderson stretched out on his couch after an extended mission. As the Officer in Charge of his platoon, Grady spent most of his time gathering information and intel for the missions his men and he would carry out. However, the mission had worn him down emotionally for the past three weeks. They'd taken down Philippe Barnesto, a major player in the war on human trafficking. In all, the SEAL platoons assigned to this mission had released over three hundred and fifty women and children and had dismantled Barnesto's group using every necessary strategy.

It would be impossible for him to close his eyes any time soon. He'd need to bury the horror of the last three weeks like he always did after a mission before he'd sleep normally. It wasn't a great plan, but it seemed to work for him. Grady never took anything to help him sleep. He'd survived BUDs training in a sleep-deprived state. He refused to give in to outside help besides the good Lord's. Sleep would come when he needed it.

Grady had enlisted in the Navy at eighteen years old and had never regretted his decision. After three years with the Navy, he trained to be a SEAL and began his exclusive fight in the war on human trafficking. Six years ago, he'd been promoted to his current position. At thirty-three, he still fought the demons from his childhood. Carrying them on each mission, he used them to help eliminate the most vile offenders. He justified his actions every time he saw an innocent woman or child in captivity. Some of his missions over the years had involved releasing men and boys from debt bondage or forced labor, but an overwhelming percentage of the rescue missions had been to release women and children from sex trafficking. It made him sick to know that there was enough scum in the world for his and numerous other SEAL platoons to solely dedicate their lives to protecting others against human trafficking. He'd been fighting this fight nonstop for twelve years without an end.

His eyelids were heavy sandbags; he was losing the fight against a rushing flood. The doorbell jolted him, and he sprang up, whipping his feet to the floor. *Who could that be?* He thought he'd done a good job being incognito the last few weeks. No one other than a young boy he'd met in the woods behind his rented cabin knew he was here. He'd sent his men on leave. Maybe one of them couldn't get a flight and needed to stay with him for a day or two. Grady and his men had sixty days to recover from this past soul-sucking mission unless another mission popped up, cutting the time short.

Grady had his knife in his pocket and his 9 mm tucked behind his back. But neither of those weapons prepared him for what was on the other side of the door.

A beautiful blonde stood holding a dish that he couldn't will his eyes to look down at. This might not be someone wanting to hurt him, but it was definitely a dangerous situation. Grady and women didn't go well together. He didn't know how to act around them. *Them?* Like women were strange sea creatures. His men liked to set him up on dates, and sometimes he went, but they always ended up the same. They teased him endlessly about his lack of flirting skills, but he'd never felt the need to flirt.

Getting close to a woman had never fit into his life. He'd never be like his dad and leave, but a woman could leave him and take their child away or leave him to raise a kid alone. He or other boys from the group home had experienced all those scenarios. *No, thank you.* His SEAL buddies were his family, and that's all he needed. Now, the idea of leaving a wife behind as a widow left him feeling too guilty to try. Besides, he should have been married six years ago but was too cowardly to go through with it. For one of his late SEAL brothers, he'd agreed to marry a woman he'd never even seen a picture of.

"Can I help you?" he asked, finally finding his voice. But before she could respond, he heard footsteps rushing towards them. He whipped out his Glock 19—the best 9 mm, in his opinion—and shielded her with his body. He wrapped an arm behind him, holding her there to protect her from the approaching danger.

Scanning the area, his vision caught on two figures. Suddenly, he felt a hot breath on his neck. The woman behind him forcefully whispered, "Those are my children. Please put the gun away before you scare them to death!" Her voice's protectiveness and close proximity filled his chest with an unfamiliar warmth.

The look of terror in the kids' eyes made his gun disappear. He released the tension from his shoulders and sidestepped, revealing their mother.

"See. I told you he was tough, Avery." The boy's words made Grady almost smile.

Avery shrugged.

Thomas took a step toward Grady. "You're like Rambo, but not as big. Taller, maybe that's why you seemed bigger."

Harboring a mischievous smile, Avery mumbled something under her breath that Grady couldn't hear. A sharp look passed from mother to daughter. Grady was probably better off not knowing.

"How tall are you anyway?" The boy was now at his side, measuring himself against Grady. He almost reached Grady's shoulder. "Are you in the military?"

"I'm six-three, without shoes, and yes, I am."

The boy stared at him, worshiping Grady like he was a Greek god. Grady felt uncomfortable and shifted from one foot to another, rubbing his hand through his hair. The boy continued to stare. *He wasn't anything special. If he were, his dad wouldn't have left him to endure a fate Grady would never wish on any child.*

"How much do you weigh?"

"Thomas, you're asking some personal questions, and we don't even know his name," his mom gently admonished. Her angelic voice sent warm tingles through Grady's body. He'd been admonished plenty of times between his gruff foster families growing up and always having a higher-ranking officer to report to, but it had never sounded like this.

"I don't mind." Grady liked that one of the kids was a boy. He could relate to a boy. The beautiful woman, still holding the dish, was way out of his league; he didn't have a clue what to say to her. Even worse was her teenage daughter. Who in all the world knew what to say to a teenage girl? *Focus on the boy!* a voice directed him. "I weighed in at two forty on my last check."

The boy's eyes widened. "Maybe you are Rambo. He was only five-ten; one ninety-seven. You must be way tougher than Rambo!" Looking at his mom, he asked, "Don't you think so?"

The blonde's flawless cheeks blushed. *What did that mean? What did he want it to mean?* He'd been in dangerous situations all his life, but none as alarming as the situation he found himself in now. He couldn't help but stare at her sea green eyes. They shone bright like the sun, yet there was a haunting look that he'd seen on too many of his SEAL buddies' faces. Still, those beautiful eyes. . .

She ignored her son's questions and pushed the dish toward Grady. "My son told me we had a new neighbor in the cabin. Sorry, it took me so long to come and welcome you. We live right through the woods on the path if you ever need anything. Unfortunately, we made cookies. I can't imagine anyone that looks as good as you would eat cookies. I mean, SEALs train hard, so I imagine cookies aren't on your approved food list." Her face burned with embarrassment.

Grady bit back a grin. A light breeze hit him in the face. Her sweet, fruity scent with a hint of spice left him with a strong desire to move closer to the fit blonde occupying his little porch and soak in her scent.

"Thomas can be a bit overzealous with military men, something he aspires to be, so if he's ever…too much…please don't feel bad telling him to back off a bit."

"That's right. I've got six more years, then I'll be off to fight like my dad," Thomas interrupted.

Grady lifted the plate in acknowledgment. "Thank you."

"No. Thank you for your service." The blonde pointed toward the teenage girl. "That's Avery. She's always listening to music. She dreams day and night about becoming a singer, so she's always listening to her headphones. I think she uses them to shut out the world, but what do I know? I'm just Mom."

Grady let a small smile escape. He liked her carefree yet direct manner. *Was her rambling an indication of her nervousness? Did he do that?* She made his stomach flip flop. He hadn't experienced that since he turned eighteen and signed his life over to the Navy. He hadn't thought much about his future when he'd enlisted. His dad had left him and his mom when Grady had turned two. Then, his mom had died of a brain aneurysm and left him alone at eight. He'd bounced from one foster home to another for the next ten years.

Thomas pulled Grady from his thoughts. "Our dad died on a mission, and she's mad at the world; that's why she's always listening to her music."

Grady understood completely. His heart ached for the young girl. It also made him wonder about the beauty who handed him the plate of cookies. How was she dealing with the death of her husband? His gut told him something about this situation seemed eerily familiar, and his gut was never wrong.

No matter how beautiful she was, it wouldn't matter. His past had made it nearly impossible for him to engage in a romantic relationship, so he'd never tried before, and he wouldn't start now. Besides, he was on temporary leave, further making the unfamiliar tightness in his chest a reason to avoid this woman. His life belonged to protect and serve—a SEAL for about two more years until he retired. Then, he'd probably work private security to save people from, or prevent, human trafficking.

He directed his attention to Thomas's mother and asked something he shouldn't have. "I'm so sorry. How long ago?" He never asked questions, keeping to himself to avoid connections with anyone outside of his inner circle of SEAL brothers, but the gnawing ache in his gut couldn't prevent him from wanting to get to know the woman in front of him.

"Thank you. Six years ago. He was a hero fighting the war on human trafficking."

Grady steeled himself. "So he was a SEAL?"

The woman shook her head proudly, but her face filled with anguish. Grady had learned to control his body language and his facial expressions. If her husband had died as she said, then he may have known him. First, he had to know this woman's name. "I'm sorry you got left behind..." He waited for her to fill in her name.

"Olivia."

He wished she would have given him a last name, but he didn't blame her for being careful. In fact, he appreciated her precaution. He'd seen the effects of careless women too many times, and the thought of having to rescue the group standing in front of him from traffickers made him cringe.

"I'm Grady Gunderson." He reached out his hand. Olivia's face turned white, and her jaw dropped before she quickly snapped it shut as she placed her hand in his. "Is everything okay?"

She stumbled on her words. "G-Grady Gunderson?"

His smile faltered. She pulled her hand from his; instantly, he longed to feel the warmth of it inside his palm again. Then, as quickly as she had pulled her hand away, she bounded down the steps.

"Come on, kids. Leave this SEAL to his cookies and let him rest. He doesn't get much time off."

Grady wondered what caused the woman and her daughter to bolt. They were gone in a flash, but Thomas lingered. He asked Grady if he would share his military training with him so he could prepare himself to follow in his dad's footsteps.

Before he could answer, Avery appeared with her hand on her hip. "Thomas, Mom said you need to come right now."

"Go on, Buddy. When I return the plate, we can see what your mom says about that." Grady would have thought he gave the boy a million bucks by the way he smiled at him.

Stepping back into the house, Grady placed the cookies on the counter. Olivia was right; he didn't eat cookies very often, but he had an unexplained desire to do just that for her. He took a bite, and it melted in his mouth. Sensations exploded like he was eight years old again, eating Pop Rocks. He hadn't had a cookie in that long, or the thought of returning the plate to the brilliant baker excited him more than he'd thought.

A pit formed in his stomach. How could this woman affect him so quickly? He wanted to know more about her. She'd started to break through the walls he'd developed long ago to protect himself. With how Olivia had just reacted, she clearly didn't like him, which definitely wouldn't work out in his favor.